The Glory Road

"Think where man's glory
most begins and ends,
And say my glory was I
had such friends."

William Butler Yeats

Printed in the United States of America. For information, address Finns Way Books™, 360 Grand Avenue, Suite 204, Oakland, California, 94610; or contact www.finnswaybooks.com

For information on Finns Way Reading Group Guides, please contact Finns Way Books™ by electronic mail at readinggroupguides@finnswaybooks.com

The Glory Road is a work of fiction. Each and every character is entirely the work of the imagination or is used fictionally. Any similarity to people living or deceased is coincidental.

ISBN 978-0-9985288-0-9

March 27, 2017

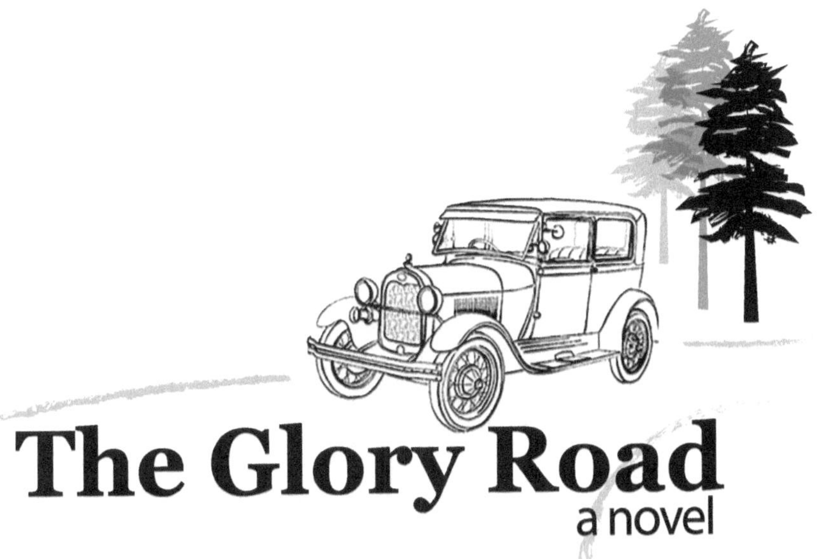

The Glory Road

a novel

Bruce Coyle

The Glory Road

1

Everything changed the summer I turned fifteen. The day it happened began pretty much like any other. Momma and Daddy got up before daylight, as usual, got me up, too, and we all went down to the cookhouse about sunup. Waters and Daddy drank coffee and talked, the way they always did. When breakfast was ready, I ate in the kitchen while the dining hall filled with the thumping of loggers' boots on the oiled wood floor and the clatter of plates and cups on tables and the scraping of silverware on thick china. Over all that commotion were the gruff voices of the men themselves, bragging, complaining, laughing, starting another day in their lives about the same way as always.

When the men had clomped outside, and Waters and Daddy had gone off to work with them, Momma made me stay in for another two hours for what she called my "schoolin'." There wasn't any real school within miles, and there weren't but four children in the whole logging camp, but Momma insisted we needed to be able to read and write and count. She had found out that one of the other cooks, Miss Garvey, had tried teaching once, and that was good enough for Momma.

Each morning from September to June, Momma got the four of us together and between breakfast and dinner Miss Gravy (as we called her to ourselves) would hold dominion over the two Barnhart sisters, Dottie and Dora, Fuzzy Nichols, and me.

Fuzzy's real name was Forrest Redfield Nichols, way too big a name for someone our age to carry around, although Miss Gravy seemed to like the sound of it, since she always called him by all three names — especially when she thought he'd done something wrong, which was often. But I just called him Fuzzy, and I was always Just', instead of Justin, which Miss Gravy insisted upon. Miss Gravy seemed to prefer the company of Dottie and Dora, her being a girl herself evidently making her more comfortable among her own kind.

She did manage to teach Fuzzy and me to count and do sums and the like. She also taught us to read some, but her tastes ran to Bible stories and "po-ems" about cute little animals and stories about girls who played with dolls and gave tea parties on the lawn. She was using her own books to teach us, and they apparently didn't have much in the way of stories of adventure in faraway places, or of boys who did heroic things against all odds. But most of the time Fuzzy and me put up with it and left to have our adventures on our own when Miss Gravy let us go.

One day, after the dinners had been boxed and sent up the track to the men in the woods and the noon whistle blew at the mill to signal that it was time to eat, Fuzzy and I gave up looking for arrowheads and fool's gold in the creek below the mill and made our way back to the cookhouse to get our dinner, too. After we'd washed up outside and wiped our feet, we settled in at the little table in the kitchen. Our dinner was leftover breakfast wedged between thick slices of bread — bacon and fried egg sandwiches toasted on the stove. On the other side of the kitchen wall, the dining hall buzzed with the chatter of the mill workers and the usual rattle of plates and cups and the scraping of boots on the wooden floor.

After a while, I thought I could hear something else, a sound that didn't belong to the usual cookhouse noise.

"Listen," I said to Fuzzy, "do you hear that?"

"Hear what?" Fuzzy said, a little egg yolk dripping from the corner of his mouth. "I don't hear nothing."

"Listen—there it is again. Sounds like a bell, but far off."

Fuzzy cocked his head, listening. "Yeah—I hear it, too. Sounds like it's coming from back in the woods somewhere."

Pretty soon everybody must have heard it, 'cause all the talk in the dining hall suddenly stopped. The ringing was louder, now, a steady single clang, like a church bell, rung at regular intervals, getting closer all the time. The mill hands put down their cups and forks, and their boots scraped the floor as they all made their way outside. The cooks left off their work, and Momma and Fuzzy and me all went outside, too. We stood on the steps of the cookhouse and watched.

Across the way, the men gathered by the loading dock, looking back into the woods where the sound was coming from. Soon we could hear the chuff of the little Gypsy engine and the insistent ringing of its brass bell. Coupled to the locomotive was a single flatcar. When it got close enough, the men rushed forward to see. Sitting on the flatcar with his back to the crowd was a tall black man, holding another man against his chest as the train slowed to a stop.

"Stay here. Don't move," Momma told me. She looked at me, and her eyes were wide with fear. "Just stay here, Justin. You understand?"

I understood, all right. I knew what I saw. Waters was sitting on that flatcar, holding Daddy in his arms. And no one had to tell me—Daddy was dead.

Momma slowly made her way through the crowd of men, holding her hand to her mouth. The crowd of men parted like the sea for Israel, and Momma walked between them. She climbed onto the log car, and Waters helped her up to sit with Daddy. Momma put her hand to Daddy's bloodied cheek, smoothed back the hair from his forehead. She looked down at him for a long time. When she sat back, Waters put his arm around her. She leaned into his chest and sobbed.

The shock of Daddy's death pulled the rug out from under me. I remembered him sitting on the cookhouse steps having his morning coffee with Waters. The steam drifted up from their coffee mugs as they talked and joked with each other in the crisp morning air. Three hours later he was gone from us forever, his spirit whisked away like that steam.

It was a while before I could put together what happened, but it turned out to be a typical woods accident, one of the dozens of accidents that claimed a logger's arm or leg or life from time to time. Widow-makers fell from trees, axes slipped, trees jumped stumps and fell the wrong direction; there were many ways for things to go wrong.

Waters and Daddy had been setting chokers. Other men were felling trees, and the trees landed upslope and down, sometimes in a tangle, mixed in with branches knocked loose from other trees as they fell to the ground. The choker setters went in while the tree was still "live" and, therefore, dangerous. They wrapped the cable, or choker, around the fallen tree and fastened it so it could be yarded by the Gypsy, which had an attached spool and cable, to the landing, where it would be bucked to length and loaded onto the log cars. Sometimes the trees rolled over the men before they could be secured. This time Waters and Daddy were setting the chokers. When they were set, the whistle punk signaled the yarder, and the choker setters got out of the way as fast as they could, and the cable pulled the tree up the hill. Daddy had just finished setting the choker and leaped out of the way. But when the engine took up the slack, the cable had snapped under the strain and flung itself back down the hill, the ragged end whipping back and hitting Daddy, knocking him down. The log had slid back down the hill, rolling over Daddy and killing him instantly.

It was the kind of accident you heard about from time to time, something that usually happened to someone you barely knew, but Daddy's death changed everything.

2

Momma and Daddy and me were living in Cooper's Gulch, a little sawmill town in the hills. There wasn't much to it, wasn't really a town at all, just the mill, big and sprawling, spreading to suit its own needs in a little valley shoved up against the base of the hills where the redwood trees huddled close together and pointed green fingers into the sky.

A creek ran down from the hills, and the builders of the mill had dammed it with piles of earth and big wooden floodgates to make a pond to hold the logs before they were fed into the mill. Beside the mill was a long loading dock, with a landing on one side, where the little work locomotive came down from the hills and dumped its load of logs into the pond. On the other side of the dock there was another railroad track for the big Heisler locomotive that came to hook up the loads of cut lumber and haul them twenty miles to a town on the coast where they would be shipped to places all over the world.

The mill superintendent and his foremen lived in the only real house in the town, a two-story affair near the mill with offices on the lower floor and living space above. Most of the men who worked in the woods stayed in rough skid shacks lined up beside each other along the railroad track, but some of the men who worked in the mill year-round stayed in cabins built on the hillside above the mill. A little company store down the track a ways sold personal items like tobacco, various tonics and medicines, boots and stockings, long-handled underwear, and other necessities. There was a blacksmith shop beside it and a smith that repaired wagon wheels and tools and the occasional automobile. He made simple hardware items for the mill, hinges and hooks and the like.

Further down the track on a little spur, there was a turntable for the locomotives, a big round pit with a bridge across the middle. The bridge had wheels on each end that rolled on a track at the edge of the pit. The engine was driven onto the bridge rails, and men with long poles pushed against the engine, turning it around to face the opposite direction.

Another track led from the turntable to an ash pit, where locomotives' fireboxes were cleaned out, and beyond that was a repair shop where work was done on the engines when it was needed. The shop had tracks that ran all the way into the building with open pits below, where men with greasy overalls scrabbled down with hand lanterns to work on the undersides of engines and cars. The engine could be run all the way inside the building, and there were tall wooden doors on the front of the building that were closed when the weather turned cold.

The cookhouse was set a ways off from the mill on the other side of the loading dock. Momma worked there, helping to cook the big meals that were prepared every day for the loggers and mill workers. Momma came from Ireland, came on the promise of work made by her Uncle Hal, who was one of the mill foremen. Her name was Molly Moran, and she had dark hair and very pretty pale skin that blushed so easily that Daddy always said she had roses in her cheeks.

When she first arrived, Uncle Hal got her settled in at the cookhouse, where she stayed in one of the rooms upstairs that were provided for the occasional bigwigs who showed up at the mill and for the few women who worked there.

The cookhouse itself was a long, white-painted building with a shingled roof. The dining hall took up almost all of the downstairs, with long rows of tables laid from end to end on the oiled wood floor. There was an entrance at one end of the dining hall. To the side of the door was a stairway leading to the rooms upstairs. At the other end of the dining hall two doorways led into the kitchen at the back of the building. The kitchen had two outside doors, one on each side, that could be opened to let in cool air when it got too hot. A cast iron stove set in red bricks took up most of the space along the back wall. A shiny nickel-plated rail lined the front of the stove and fancy trim around the warming racks above it stood out against the black iron. A round plaque on the front said "J. G. Ils Mfg. Co," and Uncle Hal said it had been shipped all the way up the coast from San Francisco.

The cooks got up before daylight to fire up the big stove, brewing endless pots of coffee, cooking big pans of oatmeal, and frying mountains of bacon and eggs, potatoes, and flapjacks. When the loggers were settled and the food was ready, Momma and Miss Garvey carried the big platters into the dining hall, parading through the open doors. Because she was younger and prettier, Momma got a lot of attention from the timber bucks, whistle punks, and such who took their meals there.

Momma's Uncle Hal had promised his sister that he would look out for her daughter, and he did, but probably not in the way she had expected. Before he got older and settled in as a foreman at the mill, Uncle Hal had done a lot of things. He had started out years earlier as a river pig, guiding rafts of logs down the rivers. He had been a bullwhacker in places that still logged with oxen. He was good with animals, but not so good with people. He was gruff and cranky and always seemed like he thought every man he met would sooner or later cause him trouble.

Momma told me Uncle Hal had been married once, to an Irish girl named Orla. He had bought a ranch when he arrived from the old country, made improvements to it, built a new house to replace the little cabin that was there. Two years later, his Orla came over, and they started a new life together. But shortly thereafter Orla had died, and Hal was left alone on the ranch.

"It just took the wind out of his sails, Justin," Momma said. "My ma was his sister, and she told me what happened. She said Hal was a good man who had known hard times and given up on his dream. I know she was right about that. 'Tis a sad man under all that bluff and swagger, but a good one. One day you'll come to see that, I hope."

Uncle Hal didn't have much to say most of the time, especially to me. He wore a wide, sweat-stained hat over his bald head and carried a bullwhip when he walked about the mill. Most people seemed to be scared of him. I had seen him take the head off a snake from twenty feet with that whip, and I was a little afraid of him myself.

Momma worked in the cookhouse, and Daddy worked in the woods with his friend Waters. That was his name, just Waters. He told me he had another, but he said Waters was good enough. I sometimes called him Mr. Waters, but he didn't seem to like the sound of that, either. Mostly, I just called him Waters like everybody else did.

Billy Coulter was Daddy's name, and he and Waters had worked their way to California from Oklahoma in an old Model T Ford truck they owned together. They did all kinds of work, whatever they could find along the way. They were quite a pair, Waters and my father. They attracted plenty of attention, and often a little trouble, wherever they went. Mostly it was because Waters was a Negro, and my daddy wasn't. Certain folks seemed to take offense just by seeing them together. Of course, when you knew them as I did, they were just people, two of the finest people I ever knew.

Daddy said Waters was the only man he ever truly trusted. They had started off working together in Oklahoma and decided for some reasons I didn't really understand to try their luck in California. I grew up listening to their stories about their travels, how they worked together, the kinds of jobs they'd had, how they stuck together even after their truck threw a rod and gave up the ghost, and they had to hoof it along the road for a while. When they tried to hitch a ride, most people just passed them by, but eventually they met up with someone who let them ride in the back of his truck, and they made it to California. They fared better than the Okies who followed them years later when the drought and the dust storms took off the topsoil and so many folks got tractored off their lands and headed west to look for work.

Sometimes they missed out on jobs 'cause they wouldn't take a job unless both of them got hired. It made Daddy hopping mad when people treated them that way. He said they were a team, whether other folks liked it or not, and their work spoke for itself. It was those other folks who had a problem.

Daddy was a small man, but stocky, with strong shoulders and muscles that stood out on his arms when he worked. Waters was tall and slim and powerfully built, but graceful and quick in his movements. If they'd been horses,

Waters said, Daddy was strong enough to pull the plow, but he'd be the one to win the race.

When they finally got to California, they took whatever jobs they could find. Eventually they came to Cooper's Gulch and settled in, working in the woods during the good weather months and in the sawmill when it ran during the winter. They always worked together, even after Daddy met my mother.

It didn't take much more than a look from Uncle Hal to put most men in their places, but when Momma took a liking to Daddy, she somehow managed to get around Uncle Hal's orneriness long enough to figure out she and Daddy were meant for each other, and they said their "I do's" in a meadow by the river on a sunny afternoon in May, as most of the camp looked on. Momma and Daddy moved to the little cabin on the hill, where I showed up the next year.

Waters and Daddy still worked together in the woods, and Momma kept on in the cookhouse. She liked to tell me stories about how she took me to the cookhouse with her each morning and parked me in a basket in a corner near the big iron stove that lined the back wall. I don't remember any of that, of course, but Momma said I didn't cause much trouble as a baby. She said the kitchen was always warm, full of the good smells of wood smoke, sizzling bacon, and steaming coffeepots and noisy with the clamor of kettles and the clanking of the big oven doors–all of which apparently kept me occupied and happy.

Waters and Daddy always met up at the cookhouse early in the morning and went off to the woods with the other men after breakfast. They waited by the railroad track next to the mill, standing there in their "corked boots" and waist overalls with the legs cut short, held up by black suspenders.

They stood with the other men who chewed tobacco and spat brown streams onto the dirt. Some of them rolled cigarettes from the Bull Durham pouches they carried in their denim work shirt pockets with the tag hanging by a string from the flap. In the cool morning air their heads were wreathed in the warm moisture of their breath and little clouds of cigarette smoke that drifted around them. When the Gypsy locomotive backed down the track by the millpond, they climbed aboard the log cars, the whistle blew, the steam hissed from the smokebox, and the little engine carried the men into the woods. Momma and I stood on the porch of the cookhouse and waved until the cars were out of sight.

At night after supper, Momma and Daddy liked to sit out on the steps and talk. When I was little, Momma would tell me a story or sometimes read from a book before bedtime. Then she would sing me a song, usually a song from her growing up days, and sometimes Daddy sang, too, if he knew the song. Daddy had a fine singing voice, but mostly he liked to listen to Momma sing.

Sometimes Waters came to our cabin in the evening. He and Daddy often sat on the steps, joking with each other, talking about this and that. On Saturday nights when most of the other men went off drinking or headed into town to look for other kinds of entertainment, Waters usually came to have supper with us. I heard him tell Momma once that he never got tired of her cooking or her company, which, of course, made her blush, but when I was a little older, after I'd been put to bed one night, I overheard him telling them about the last time he'd gone off to town by himself.

"There was a couple guys I thought were okay— bought a bottle with money we chipped in together. 'Course I couldn't go in and sit down with them to drink it, but they said it was all right. They would come outside, and we would go down by the river where there was a little park and we could find a nice place to sit and have a drink, maybe play some cards or pitch horseshoes.

"Well, they went into the bar and bought the bottle, and we headed down to this spot one of the guys, name was Clarence, said he knew about. When we got there, we were passing that bottle around, just talking, y' know, having a nice time together. About twenty minutes later, six big guys from the bar showed up carrying axe handles, told the other men they were going to show 'em what comes of drinking with 'niggers' and proceeded to go at them with the axe handles. Clarence got busted up pretty bad. Then they turned on me, knocked me out. When I came to, I was alone on the ground with a bloody knot on the side of my head. That was the last time I went to town by myself."

Daddy said, "Lucky for them it wasn't you and me together that night. Remember that place in Fresno?" I drifted into sleep as he and Waters began telling Momma another of their stories.

When I was about seven or eight, Daddy and Waters pooled their money and bought a car. It was a Model A Ford sedan, and there was just room in it for Momma and Daddy and Waters and me. It made me feel kind of special, since only a few of the people who stayed in Cooper's Gulch owned a car. Some of the men who went to town at the end of the week caught a ride on the train when it hauled its last load if they could. Others tried to get a ride with somebody who had a car. One of the foremen, a single man named Harley Yates, had a stake truck with a canvas cover over the back, and he usually filled up the back, charging fellows a dollar to take them to town and bring them back on Sunday night.

Sometimes on Sundays Momma and Daddy and

Waters and me all went for a ride along one of the country roads. Momma always packed up a hamper with cold chicken or sandwiches, and maybe a pie or some potato salad. We'd find a nice place, usually by the river or in a redwood grove, and have a picnic lunch. It was nice to get away from the mill and have a change of scenery. After we ate, Momma and Daddy and Waters sat and talked, but I usually got bored and went exploring. Momma always told me, "Don't you go wanderin' off, now," but I wanted to poke around and see what I could find. I never got lost, and I always stayed close enough to hear Momma call me when it was time to go.

Sometimes Daddy and Waters went down to the river with me, and we'd skip stones across a pool. I always spent time picking just the perfect stone, round and flat, not too big. I pinched it tight between my thumb and forefinger, the weight of it resting on my middle finger curled underneath. Then I bent slightly to my right, and launched a sidearm toss that sent it spinning across the pool, just above the surface of the water. If I did it just right, I was rewarded by seeing it skip two or three times before it sank out of sight. After considerable practice, I was starting to get the hang of it, but Daddy and Waters always put me to shame.

One time when I was still little, Momma and Daddy took me to town to see a carnival that was appearing there. They were "all foxed up," Uncle Hal said, when he saw them in their Sunday clothes. Momma had on her best dress—a pale blue one, with lace on the collar. She topped it off with a white straw hat that had a matching blue band and a sprig of lavender cornflowers on the side. She was beautiful in that outfit.

Daddy was decked out in a gray suit that made him look elegant, so different from the chambray shirt, cut-off overalls, and corked boots I was used to seeing. When he put on the pearl gray hat he kept for special occasions, I knew it would be a great day just by looking at them.

On the way to town, Daddy told us how he and Waters had worked in a carnival one time during their travels to California. He said they stood outside the lot when the carnival was setting up, and they got picked to work for the day. They unloaded trucks, helped put together rides and set up the joints the carnies used for their "skin" games, as Daddy called them, places where you tried to win prizes at games of skill. Daddy said skill didn't matter much, since most of the games were rigged, and you usually got "skinned" and lost your money.

"They worked us hard all day. A young guy, part of the crew putting up the rides, came over to us in the beginning, told us 'Whatever you do, don't sit down. Boss'll fire your ass if he thinks you're loafin'. You can lean on something if there's a break in the work, but don't sit down.' Turned out to be good advice. Even though the carnies were a rough-looking bunch, we never had any trouble.

"Waters got pretty steamed when one of those guys tried to hire him to be in their African dodger set-up, but he held his temper 'cause we needed the money. We worked a long day, got paid at the end, and moved on."

"What's an African dodger?" I asked from the back.

"It's an awful game where they get a Negro man to stick his head out through a hole in a canvas sheet so people can throw a ball at his head. Got a jungle scene painted on the canvas. Sometimes the man's head looks like it's coming out of an alligator's mouth. 'Hit the nigger baby in the head – win a seegar!' You can imagine how Waters took to that."

"That's so awful," Momma said. "I don't know how he could stand for that."

"Like I said, we were broke and needed the money."

"Justin, you forget what you just heard. "Tis shameful, the things some people do to others."

"You're right about that, Molly," Daddy said. "But not all these places are like that. Let's go in, see what they've got. We'll have a good time."

When we got to the lot where the carnival was set up, Daddy parked the car, and we got in the line at the ticket booth. Daddy bought our tickets, and we went inside. We walked down a row of 'line joints'—booths connected to each other on each side—and looked at the skin games. There was one where you could win a prize by throwing a ball at three stacked-up milk bottles and knocking them all down.

"Those bottles are metal," Daddy said. "Weighted at the bottom. Give you three tries, but the balls're too soft to knock 'em over, especially the heavier ones on the bottom."

We walked along, looking at all the games. There was one where you tossed coins onto flat plates, hoping to make one stick on top or fall into other dishes stacked around. If it landed on the big flat plate, you could win a teddy bear, or if it fell into a cup or vase you could keep the dish and take it home. Momma said, "I want to try that. It doesn't look too hard."

Daddy gave her a few dimes to try. She gave him her handbag to hold, put a dime in her hand, and tossed it lightly toward the big flat plates on top. The dime hit the first plate, bounced over to another, then slid off the edge and fell down between the littler cups and vases. She tried it again, but the results were the same.

"Once more," she said. She gave it a toss, and it fell off the top again, but bounced from one little dish to another, finally landing in a small upturned vase. Momma was delighted.

"That was fun. Probably could buy that vase for less

than I spent, but it was fun tryin' to win it that way." She looked up at Daddy and smiled. When she took back her handbag, she looped her arm in his and stood on her tiptoes to kiss his cheek.

There were different shows set up along both sides of what Daddy called the Midway, with big pictures painted on canvas sheets advertising the sights to be seen if you paid to go behind the curtain. We walked along, looking at the pictures. There were men Daddy called barkers who stood outside and gave speeches trying to get people to come inside and see the shows.

There was a freak show behind a big curtain painted with scary pictures of cows with two heads, a pair of Siamese twins, and what looked like just the top half of a lady sitting on a three legged table. She didn't have any arms or legs and looked like somebody had parked her on that table just like she was a vase or a candlestick. There was a picture of a giant and a man in a leopard skin who was supposed to be a cannibal from the jungles of Borneo. The barker said he would bite the heads off live chickens, though I couldn't imagine why anyone would want to see that. A Chinese man stood out front wearing a long robe with a cone-shaped hat on his head, and the barker promised that the man's own head was just as pointy when he took off the hat.

Daddy said there were different kinds of freaks in those shows. Some were born freaks, who were deformed by nature, some were made freaks, like a tattooed lady, and some were gaffed freaks, fakes like that cannibal from Borneo who just pretended to be what they said. Daddy wanted to go inside, but I was too scared. Momma hugged me close and said it was okay, but I felt like I had let Daddy down. I always wished I'd gone in there to see what was inside.

The main attraction was a lion tamer named Clyde

Beatty. We all wanted to see that show. Daddy got us tickets from the booth outside a big white tent where there was a big banner with a picture of a snarly lion face-to-face with Beatty, who was dressed in white with a jungle helmet on his head. We went inside and got seats in the fourth row, high enough to see the show, but still close to the action.

Clyde Beatty came in through a door in the big metal cage and locked it behind him. He was about Daddy's size, smaller than someone like Waters, but slim and kind of stocky, with good-sized shoulders. He carried a whip in one hand and had a pistol strapped to his side. An announcer introduced him, saying how brave and fearless Mr. Beatty was and telling us we needn't be afraid.

Clyde raised his arms in the air, holding his whip in his right hand, and looked at the audience. After we all clapped and cheered, there was a trumpet fanfare, and he turned his back to us and signaled to a man outside the back of the cage who pulled down a lever that let in the lions.

The big cats padded around in the cage, snarling and tossing their heads from side to side, and Clyde used his whip and a chair to get them under control. He got them to parade around the cage and then made them jump up onto platforms that stood along the back wall of the cage. Some of them got balky and charged at him, but he cracked his whip at them and a couple of times he fired his pistol in the air. It was exciting to see him make them perform. We all gasped when one big lion with a shaggy mane growled and swiped at Beatty with his paw, but he held the chair in front of himself and walked right up to the lion. He cracked the whip and made the cat back down. It gave me shivers just watching. When he finally got them all lined up, the lions chuffed and roared and made me glad I was on the other side of the cage. He put on a good show, and everybody cheered when it was over.

After Clyde Beatty, the next best thing was a sideshow called The Wall of Death. It was a big round wooden tank like a water tank. When you bought your ticket, you climbed up some stairs to a platform that went all around the top of the tank where you could look down inside. There was a door in the wall at the bottom, and a man came in the door and got on an Indian motorcycle parked nearby. He got it started and revved up the noisy motor. Then he rode round and round in the bottom of that tank. He went faster and faster till he went up a little slope between the floor and the side of the tank, and then he climbed up the wall going around faster still. There was a white line painted just below the top, and he got real close to the line as he spun higher and higher. It looked like he could fly out over the top any minute. It was loud and smoky and a little bit scary, but everyone loved it.

I would never forget that day. It was the most fun, something special we all enjoyed together that would never happen again.

Momma finally started letting me go by myself to meet Daddy when the log train brought the men back to the mill in the afternoons. I waited at the end of the loading dock until I could hear the Gypsy off in the distance chugging toward the mill, puffs of steam appearing now and then through the trees. When I heard the whistle blow, I could see it coming down the hill toward the loading dock, where it finally came to a grinding halt in a rush of steam and smoke. The men got down from the cars, dirty and tired-looking, their legs unfolding stiffly as they stepped off on their corked boots. When I saw my Daddy, I ran to him and jumped up so he could put me on his shoulders. Then, because he knew I wanted him to, he always carried me down to the end of the dock, so we could watch the logs being unloaded into the pond. It was exciting, and I never got tired of watching as the huge redwood logs, with their thick, shaggy bark, rolled off the cars and down the ramp into the log pond, where they landed with a big splash that came right up onto the dock. Later, when the logs had all been unloaded, the pond monkeys, with their long Peavey hooks, wrestled the big logs into some kind of order so they could be lined up and sent into the mill. The logs twisted and rolled sometimes, but the pond monkeys soon got them straightened out.

When I got too big to be put up on his shoulders, Daddy took my hand and walked with me to the end of the dock so we could watch them unload the logs. "Don't want you to fall in, do we?" He said. Daddy's hands were rough, the skin toughened by hard work and lined with dirt when he came home from work. I always felt safe when he held my hand in his.

I had outgrown the need for hand-holding before he died, at least in Daddy's mind. When he stepped down from the log train at the end of those last days, we walked over to watch the logs splash into the pond, and we stood beside each other to watch. He always put his hand on my shoulder as we stood there. For a while after Daddy died, I went down to the landing in the afternoon when the train returned. I stood off to one side, watching the men step down from the train, Waters with them, but by himself just the same. At times I thought I felt Daddy's hand on my shoulder.

The summer I turned twelve, Daddy brought home a spotted fawn he had come across in the woods. Its mother had been killed, and he had found the fawn near the mother's body, weak and starving. He knew it wouldn't make it on its own, so he carried it home in his arms, and Momma set about caring for it.

"Such a wee one as that will die without his mother's love. I know just what to do," she told Daddy. She cut a finger from a rubber glove and fastened it to an old bottle she filled with milk so that the fawn could nurse. At first its spindly legs quivered and could barely hold him up, but it soon recovered its strength, and it wasn't long before it followed her everywhere she went.

Momma worried that something would happen to that deer when it got older and began to wander further from her. It was a buck, and Momma was afraid somebody, maybe even one of the loggers or millworkers, would shoot it when it got older.

"Not much you can do about that, is there Molly?" Daddy asked.

"Sure, and there is", Momma said. "I've been thinkin' on it for some time now."

"And what have you decided then?"

"When he gets bigger, and those fine horns begin to sprout, I'm going to tie a flag around his neck so everyone will know not to shoot him. I'm goin' to call him Flag. That will be his name."

And that's just what she did. For several seasons after that, when his horns grew out, Momma tied an American flag around his neck during hunting season so that hunters would know he was her pet deer. Flag looked a little funny, but you could tell he was a pet from far away.

3

After the accident, Momma got up every morning before daylight as she always had. I went with her to the cookhouse as usual, fetched wood and water, and ate breakfast in the kitchen. But there was an emptiness about everything that made it like wandering about in the fog. Waters came in every morning, and he and Momma sat for a while on the steps outside the kitchen, talking quietly. I never knew what they talked about, but I knew it was good for Momma. I sat with her on the steps of the cabin every night, and sometimes she would sing to me one of her sad Irish songs, but I knew I was not much help to her. I was not old enough to understand what had happened to me, and I was not able to understand what was happening to her.

Waters would leave, then, and join the others as they waited for the Gypsy to build up a head of steam and carry them into the woods. But Waters stood apart from the other men now; he didn't have Daddy to stand with him, and he, too, seemed lost. As he left the cookhouse steps and walked toward the other men, I noticed that some of them stared at him and spat tobacco juice at their feet.

As the days passed, we went on as well as we could. Momma worked in the cookhouse, and I endured the attempts of Miss Gravy to teach me what she could. Everyone was unusually nice to Momma and me, as if they were tiptoeing around our feelings. Fuzzy and I still tried to think up adventures together, but I had lost interest in searching for arrowheads and fool's gold, and tormenting frogs just didn't seem right any more. The days turned into weeks and then into months. There were wouldn't be any more Sunday drives with picnic lunches, no more trips to see the circus. The wall of death was all around us now. Waters still came over for supper on Saturdays as he had before, and after we ate, he and Momma went for walks together while I stayed at the house. I knew that they were Daddy's two best friends and that somehow they would help each other find what they needed.

Uncle Hal was there, too, his presence comforting, I suppose, but his silent manner did little to change what had happened. One day he took me on a tour of the mill and showed me how the logs were made into lumber. I saw how the logs were loaded onto the headrig and heard the whine of the bandsaw as the carriage moved the log into the blade, cutting huge slabs from each log and then returning to make another pass. He showed me the filing room upstairs in the mill, where filers sharpened and set the teeth on the long, looping blades that sat on big racks that stretched across the room. He showed me the dock where men with cranes loaded the lumber, mostly thick cants and flitches that would be hauled by the big Heisler locomotive to the port, where they would be shipped to faraway places and made into lumber to build houses and other things.

It was all very interesting, and I knew Uncle Hal was spending the time with me to take my mind off things and make me feel better, but his attention was just a distraction and did little to lift my spirits.

Flag had grown into a splendid young buck. Every year he had grown, and we watched his horns become bigger with each season. This summer his velvet-covered horns had been the best so far. When he had shed the velvet, he had transformed into a fine buck with three points on each side and eyeguards as well, the smaller points that rose from the base of each horn.

In the fall he became wary and skittish, but he still remembered us. He usually came to the cookhouse in the mornings. After the men had their breakfast and left for work, when it was quiet again in the cookhouse, we went outside to look for him. The cookhouse stood in a clearing, and we often saw him at the forest edge, standing under the trees. He would raise his head and turn toward us, looking over his shoulder, those wonderful horns standing proud above his head.

He let Momma pet him and took treats from her hand with his soft nose and his pink raspy tongue. He didn't like her to touch his horns, but he let her tie the flag around his neck. He carried his horns carefully, his neck a little bowed, stepping cautiously with his dainty feet. During the fall mating season he was around less and less, but we still saw him from time to time, especially in the morning or evening.

It was in the fall that the trouble began. The weather had cooled, the trees were losing their leaves, and the first rains had begun. When the rain settled in for good, work in the woods would stop, and the mill would run shorter shifts, cutting the logs stockpiled during the good weather of the summer months.

The grubstake men with their pencil stubs in their pockets began to look at their notebooks and figure out how much money they had made and think about the long winter ahead. The men who had worked hard all summer and spent their money on Saturday night fun had little to look forward to. Tempers were short and arguments flared among them. Fistfights broke out sometimes, especially when they had been drinking. Some of the men still went to town at the end of the week, but often they returned in small, sullen groups that stood about, drinking and smoking and nursing their dissatisfaction with everything in general—with the weather, with the state of the country, with themselves. They needed more to think about. It didn't take long for them to find something new to take their minds off their troubles.

One morning after breakfast Momma had sent me out to the woodpile behind the cookhouse to get wood for the stove. I had brought in a few armfuls and was kneeling on the floor, stacking it in the bin alongside the stove. Three men came into the kitchen and asked to see Momma, who was scraping the long stovetop with a pumice block, preparing to oil it and wipe it down as she did after a meal. Some strands of her hair had come unpinned and clung damply to her neck. She looked up at the men standing there, impatient to get back to her work.

"And what are the likes of you about this mornin'? I've work to do, and so have you."

"We just wanted to tell you that it ain't right, ma'am," one of them said, stepping forward. "It ain't right a-tall." And he looked at her in a hard way, one eye squinting shut as he spoke.

"Say what you mean, won't you?" Momma said. "I've no idea what you're on about this mornin.'"

"It's just that we've noticed—we've seen you with that boy, that Waters. You and he spending a lot of time together— it ain't right. Some of the men are talking. Somepin' bound to happen, you don't watch out."

"Only thin' about to happen is that you're about to leave. That *man*, that Waters, was my Billy's best friend, stood by him no matter what. Most of you never had a friend like that in your life. Stop your blaggarding and get on with you now."

"Don't misunderstand, ma'am. It ain't us speaking our own minds. But other men are talking, and somepin's gonna happen. I—we just wanted you to know." With that, they turned and left, their boots clumping down the steps. Momma looked after them a while, and then turned back to cleaning the stove.

Miss Garvey had been watching the whole thing from the other side of the kitchen, where she was scrubbing pots and pans with a brush.

"Don't mind those three. They're all talk, always spreading rumors. They gossip like old ladies—think they know everything about what goes on around here. Listen, last week I heard one of them tell another fellow that the whole mill was going to shut down, and not just for the winter, either. I don't take those men seriously about anything."

"What would you do if they did close the mill? 'Tis not somethin' I care to think about, I swear. I've crossed the world half over to be here. I don't know what I'd do."

"Don't fret, Molly. They don't know what they're talking about. Besides, your uncle would take care of you. He promised his sister, you said."

"That he did, but things change. What would you do?"

"Well, I don't know, probably go back to cooking at the mission like I did before. Help with the children there, that sort of thing. They took me in once; they wouldn't be too surprised if I showed up on their porch again. Look, they gave me this medal when I left. You take it—maybe it'll bring you good luck one day." She took the chain off over her head and handed it to Momma.

"Thank you, Cora. Luck can't seem to find my door these days. I was raised Catholic, but I'm out of practice. I still send up a prayer or two, but I don't think He's listenin'. Maybe St. Christopher will lend me a hand."

"Have faith, Molly. Sometimes it's all we have. Give it

a try."

Momma slipped the chain over her head, tucking the medal inside her blouse.

A week or so later, when breakfast was over, Momma and I went out to see if Flag was around. She had an apple that she had cut up wrapped in a dish towel. We went out the back door and looked around, but Flag was nowhere to be seen. It was one of those gray overcast mornings when fog hung in the trees like bedsheets strung on a line, and it was hard to see to the forest's edge.

Momma peered, frowning. "What's that out there?" She said. "Do you see it, just there under the oak tree, where that limb is hangin' down?"

I looked where she was pointing, and there was something there, but it was too far away to tell what I saw. Momma stepped off the porch, walking toward the oak tree. Suddenly she began running toward the tree. I saw it then, too, and began running after her. Hanging in the branches of the tree, tied between the branches, was an American flag—a bloody American flag. Momma just stood there and stared at it. Then she reached up and untied it. She sat down abruptly in the grass, clutching it to her chest. She looked up at me then, and I looked back at her. Tears ran down her cheeks. I sat down beside her in the damp grass and cried, too. We sat there a long time together.

Sometimes it just seemed that everything had gone bust. After Daddy died, I didn't know what to do. Most days I just wandered off after breakfast, sometimes with Fuzzy, but mostly by myself. There was a big wooden trestle a ways down below the mill that crossed the creek and led to a cut through the hill on the other side. The hillsides were made of raw red dirt. The rain had caused the red to run down in bloody-looking streaks that made me think the earth had bled when it was cut open. I just sat on that trestle and looked at that red dirt and thought about what had happened to me and Momma and Daddy–and now to Flag. We had been ripped out of our lives, and things would never be the same.

When I was really feeling low, I climbed over the edge of the wooden ties and swung down onto the trestle bents, the big timbers that held up the deck. I straddled one of the beams and sat there, legs dangling, looking at the water below, and cried. It didn't do me any good, but I couldn't help it. Sometimes, when the train rumbled overhead with its drivers pounding, the engine chuffing, and all its weighted cars thundering and squealing above me, I just screamed.

On Saturdays, Waters came for supper as usual, but things seemed different somehow. It hadn't been the same since Daddy was gone, but something else had changed. Waters knew about Flag, of course. Momma had told him the next day while they visited on the steps outside the kitchen after breakfast. They had sat there as usual, but Momma had her head down, her hands in her lap. Waters looked at her, talking too low for me to hear. Momma looked at him and nodded once, tears on her cheeks. After a while, he touched her hand, then rose and walked away down the steps toward the mill.

Sitting on the porch after supper, I asked Momma to sing us a song. She had a wonderful voice, Momma did, and she knew a lot of songs, mostly ones she learned as a girl. They were almost always sad songs, or at least they seemed so to me.

"I don't much feel like singin', Justin," she had said that night.

"Please," I said, "And Waters can play his mouth harp, too." Waters carried a small harmonica in his shirt pocket.

Sometimes I heard him playing late at night when most folks were asleep. The music was far away then, like a train whistle far off, mournful. But he could play when folks sang, too, even if he didn't know the song. He could play along with most any song, and I had heard him play before, when Daddy was alive and Momma sang for Daddy and Waters and me.

"Oh, all right, but just one. Then you've got to go in. Waters and I will talk a little while. Then he has to go, too." Then she sang The Parting Glass. When she got to the part that said, "Goodnight and joy be with you all", we were all quiet for a while on the porch together. Then Momma shooed me off to get ready for bed, and I left them there in the dark together.

Later that night, we woke when we heard someone pounding on the door.

"Who's there?" Momma called.

"It's Hal. Open the door –now!"

Momma undid the latch, and Uncle Hal burst into the room. When Momma turned up the lantern, I could see his face was red, and he was out of breath from running up the hill.

"Get your things. We're leaving."

"What do you mean – leavin'?"

"I'll explain later. Get your things. Justin's too. We got no time to talk now."

Momma bustled about, gathering clothes and stuffing them into the bag she had brought with her from the old country. I rubbed the sleep from my eyes and threw on some clothes as she snatched up my things, too, and threw in a few pictures of her and Daddy and some keepsakes she kept on the table by her bed. There wasn't much, and it didn't take her more than a few minutes.

"What's this all about, Hal? What's happened?"

"We can talk later. We're leaving now." He grabbed her bag and went to the door. She took my hand and we followed him out.

Hal led us along the trail to the bottom of the hill. Hal lived in the two-story house near the mill, provided for the mill foremen. It looked like we were headed in that direction, but Hal kept to the shadows. We got to the house by a roundabout way, coming up on it from behind. Daddy's Model A was parked out back.

"Get in," Hal barked.

"What are you doin', Hal?" Momma said.

"Never mind—just get in!"

Momma and I did as we were told, climbing into the old Ford. Hal hit the starter. The motor sputtered, coughed, and finally caught. Just as we were about to pull away, Waters stepped from the shadows by the house. He was soaking wet. Hal said, "Open that door!" I threw open the door, and Waters jumped in, closing it behind him as Hal drove out of the shadow of the house and headed along the track toward the mill.

There was a knot of men gathered on the dock, angry by the look of them. Some held cant hooks, pike poles, and pickaroons. They stood there, blocking the way as we headed toward them. The Model A picked up speed, and we hurtled toward the crowd. The men stood their ground, but Hal never let up on the gas. When we got within a few yards, the men stepped aside. One or two who just missed being struck swung their tools at the car. They hit the car with a loud clang, but didn't cause any real damage. One man tossed a pike pole at us, but missed as we sped off down the track.

4

As we drove, Waters and Uncle Hal told us what happened. Waters was staying in one of the skid shacks along the road below the cookhouse. He had been staying alone since Momma and Daddy had gotten married. No one wanted to share a room with a black man, but there were those that resented his having the shack to himself. He had been walking along the track beside the loading dock. A group of men were sitting on the dock, smoking and joking among themselves. They'd come back from town, where they'd apparently done a considerable amount of drinking.

When they saw Waters coming along the track alone, they shouted at him, calling him names, trying to get a rise out of him. Waters kept walking along the track, trying to ignore them. As he drew nearer to the men, one of them, a mean, scrappy-looking man who wore a black hat and had a long scar that ran from just below his left eye almost to his chin, stepped in front of Waters, poking him in the chest with his finger.

"Somethin' wrong with you, boy? Ain't you heard me? Not polite to ignore somebody talkin' to you."

"No offense meant, Mister," Waters had said. "Just going back to the shack to sleep."

"Ask him where he's been," another of the men called out, stepping down from the dock.

"Don't need to ask where he's been, do we boys?" There was a murmur of agreement from the other men. "We know where he's been."

He turned back to Waters, poked him in the chest

again. "How you like it up on that hill? You and that Miss Molly get along real good, I hear."

"Know what I think?" The second man said. "I think he's gettin' more than dinner up there. I think he forgot who he is and where he belongs. Man who forgets that needs a reminder, a powerful reminder. What do you fellas think?"

There was another rumble of approval from the other men, and one by one they stepped down from the dock and surrounded Waters. One of the men had a length of rope, which they used to tie Waters' hands behind his back. Then they dragged and pushed him onto the loading dock.

"Be careful," the scar-faced man said, "Sometimes this here dock gets slippery. Be a shame if this here fella were to slip and fall into the pond, what with his hands bein' occupied an' all. Fella could fall in between those logs there, maybe slip underneath one of 'em. Be pretty hard to get back out 'thout drownin' hisself."

The men were dragging Waters to the other side of the loading dock, getting ready to pitch him into the pond when they heard the crack of Hal's bullwhip as it neatly plucked the hat from the scar-faced man's head. "You men get back now. Leave that man be. Go on, now. Git!" And he cracked the whip again, hitting one of the men in the shoulder, ripping a hole in his shirt. Blood began to seep from the wound. Holding his bleeding arm with his hand, the man pushed Waters off the dock and into the pond, then turned and ran. The other men suddenly lost their courage and hurried after him.

Hal had been making his rounds, checking on things as was his custom each evening, and he had heard the whole thing. He had fished Waters out of the pond with a pickaroon, pulling him up onto the dock and untying him, and the two had walked back along the dock in the other direction. Hal had told Waters to hide in the shadows behind his house and left him there. Then he came up the hill to get Momma and me.

Hal didn't think much of Waters, didn't think about what would happen to him after Daddy was gone, but he knew that what the men had wanted to do to Waters was wrong, and so he had stopped them. He didn't approve of the men who treated Momma badly and knew that she had to go away if he was going to protect her. The ranch that Uncle Hal had bought for him and Orla was located in some rolling foothills about sixty miles from Cooper's Gulch, and that's where he took us that night. "It's safer there," he said.

5

Uncle Hal's ranch was about as far away from any place as you could get. The nearest town was about twenty miles away, a wide spot in the road called Glory. From the looks of it, not many people "bound for Glory" had passed this way, except maybe a few hardscrabble farmers who had given up and gone off somewhere else. The house was built on the Glory Road, where two little creeks came together into one. The Glory Road ran a few miles further back into the hills and then, as if it had lost interest, faded into nothingness, a dusty path to nowhere.

The house was a catalog house he'd bought and had built on the ranch, a bungalow with clapboard siding. It had a wide front porch with a roof that was held up by pillars that were wide at the bottom and narrower at the top. There was a low sitting wall between the pillars that enclosed the porch. The house itself was small, but comfortable.

The door opened into a front room with a fireplace and a raised hearth along the left side, and beyond that, a dining room with a boxy bay window and built-in cabinets for dishes and such. The doorway beside the cabinet wall led into a big country kitchen with beaded wainscoting and wallpaper above the chair rail. A big cast iron cookstove with nickel-plated feet crouched along the wall across from an oak farm table with four pressed-back chairs pushed up to it. The window in the outside wall was framed by painted cupboards on each side, and a long drainboard below the window held an enameled sink whose taps poked out from the wall above it. A green cloth curtain on a metal rod hung below the sink between cupboards on each side.

A door at the back of the kitchen led to an indoor laundry room and a pantry that was big enough to walk into. Uncle Hal called it the hurling room 'cause a lot of things ended up there. An outside door in the hurling room opened to a small porch with steps that led down to the backyard and the woodshed.

A big bedroom with a window that looked out onto the front porch opened off the living room opposite the fireplace. A long hallway stretched from the living room to the kitchen, leading to two smaller bedrooms with a bathroom squeezed in between.

A little further down the road, past the house, was a tall, unpainted barn, with a big sliding door on one side to let in tractors and wagons and an open door on the other to let cows in for milking.

On a hill above the barn there was a cabin with board-and-batten siding and a rusty tin stovepipe pushing up through the roof. The cabin and barn had been there before the house was built. The hilltop was flat, and there were some big stumps left from a long time ago when someone had cut old growth trees to clear the land. There were the remains of an old orchard, too—twenty or thirty trees, most of them untended and overgrown.

When we arrived at the ranch, it was still dark. Hal went inside the house first, lit a couple of lamps, and let Momma and me in the door. Then he left to show Waters to the cabin on the hill. We were to stay in the house with Uncle Hal. The house had been closed up tight while he was gone. All the furniture was covered with sheets, and the rooms smelled a little musty and damp. While Hal was off with Waters, Momma pulled sheets off the furniture, took them out to the front porch, and shook the dust off them. Then she folded them carefully and brought them back in.

"Bring some of that wood in off the porch and set it on the hearth. 'Tis two coats cold in here. We need to build a fire."

I carried wood in from the porch while Momma bustled around inside the house, looking into the other rooms. I was on the second armful when Hal came back. When he saw what I was doing, he laid the logs in the fireplace with some kindling from a bucket on the hearth and lit the fire.

I found Momma in the middle bedroom. She had lit the bedside lamp and was making up the bed, fluffing up the pillow and setting it at the head of the bed.

"'Tis a nice room, Justin. You could grow into it and make it yours after a time."

We went back to the front room and stood by the fire a while. The chill had begun to fade, and I suddenly realized how tired I was. It was late, and even though I was scared and excited by all that had happened, the long ride in the car had helped me settle down a bit.

I went back to the bedroom and laid down on the bed. I could hear Momma and Hal talking in the front room, but I couldn't tell what they were saying. After a while, I got undressed and got into bed. It was cold in the room, but the bed had a heavy quilt over the blankets, and I soon warmed up. Before I fell asleep Momma came in and sat with me for a while.

"'Tis a nice house, this one. Hal and Orla had big dreams for this ranch. But it's still a nice place to be. Don't worry your head with anythin'. No matter what happens, you'll be safe here." Looking down, she held my hand in hers for a while. When she looked up at me, she said, "Mothers hold their children's hands for only a little while, but they hold their hearts forever. It's an old sayin', that. But it's true.

No matter what happens, always remember that."

That was the last thing I heard her say before I fell asleep.

When I woke up, it was daylight, and the house was empty. I pulled on some clothes and walked from room to room in the unfamiliar house, but there was no sign of anyone about. After a bit, I threw on my jacket and went outside. The Model A was gone. Momma and Uncle Hal were gone, too.

I walked down the road past the barn and up the hill to Waters' cabin. He was sitting on the porch steps. He had a pocketknife, and he was peeling an apple. He was taking his time, making a long, narrow strip that spiraled down to the floor between his feet.

"Everybody gone?" He asked.

"Yeah," I said.

"Figured as much," he said. "Been pretty quiet around here."

I hadn't really paid much attention, but it *was* really quiet. Back at the mill, the day began when the whistle blew and the machinery started up. Then there was the sound of the locomotive building up steam and then huffing and chuffing to and from all day. The noon whistle blew, and it was quiet for a while. Then the mill started up again after lunch and ran till the afternoon whistle blew and work ended for the day. The only time it was quiet was at night. Out here in the middle of nothing it was quiet as night all the time.

"They gone off somewheres," Waters said. "Didn't tell me where. Hal figures those men might come looking, and he don't want your momma around if they do. He don't want me around, neither. But he know those men fired up 'cause they seen your Momma and me together one time too many. Figures to keep us apart, make everybody happy, 'cept maybe you and your Momma and me."

"Are they coming back?"

"Your Uncle Hal coming back. He gotta watch out for you—wanna keep an eye on me, too."

Waters was right, of course. That evening Uncle Hal returned. He drove the Model A up the ramp and into the barn, sliding the big barn door shut after it. Then he came down to the house.

"Where's Momma?" I asked. "What did you do with her?"

"Don't worry," he said, "She's in a safe place."

"What do you mean? When's she coming back?"

"Someday, maybe—when the time is right. Then maybe she'll come back."

"Where is she?"

"She's in a good place, a safe place. Don't fret about her now."

"She's my Momma. Tell me where she is."

"It's best you don't know. Run along now, find something to do. Try not to think about her."

And that was that. In one night, my whole life changed—again. First, Daddy. Now Momma was gone, too. *Try not to think about her…* How was I supposed to do that? *…find something to do.* I couldn't imagine finding something to do that would keep me from thinking about Momma and where Hal could have taken her. And there wasn't a thing I could do about it.

Uncle Hal had never been much for talking, but he became even less talkative, it seemed. When he did speak to me, it was only about something going on right then or the next day, a word or two about the weather sometimes, or chores he wanted me to take care of.

I did what I was told. I stacked firewood on the porch, washed the dishes after meals, put out the trash. But I felt lost most of the time. I wandered along the road, listening to the sputter and whistle of red-wing blackbirds sitting on the fence posts and the shriek of an osprey sailing high above its perch in a burned-out redwood snag in the trees further up the hill, past Waters' cabin. I found a place below the road near the barn where the creek went around a big rock, and I sat there sometimes, thinking, turning it all over in my mind. I skipped a few stones sometimes, remembering the picnics with Momma and Daddy and Waters, but none of those things helped me do more than pass the time, pulling one day along toward the next.

Waters seemed to take the days as they came, comfortable with just himself for company, but he always had time for me when I showed up at the door of his cabin. The cabin had been built by the previous owner of the ranch. Uncle Hal had lived there while the house was being built, but the cabin was pretty primitive. The only water came from a spring further up the hill, where a water pipe came out of the hillside and a stream of water ran out into a metal trough. There was a drain near the top of the trough, and the overflow ran out through a pipe and down into a little gully below, eventually draining into the main creek that ran alongside the road. Water had to be carried by hand from the spring to the cabin. There was an outhouse in some trees behind the cabin.

The cabin had a sink and a drainboard along the north wall, and the sink just drained outside through a pipe in the wall and down into the same little gully. In the corner next to the sink a gray enameled coffee pot sat on the black cast iron stove that was used for heat and for cooking. The floor was covered with a gray linoleum sheet, but the walls and ceiling were unfinished, and the framing and the rafters were exposed. Waters had made a pantry of sorts by laying boards in between the wall studs to create shelves, where he kept a small store of tins of coffee and beans and such. He kept his flour and sugar in Mason jars with wire bails that held the glass lids down tight. There was a cold cupboard cut into the wall by the pantry shelves. It opened from the inside, but had shelves that were outside the cabin wall and screened in on the sides to let in the cool air to keep food a little longer.

In the middle of the room, two wooden chairs were pulled up to a square table with a green oilcloth cover. A kerosene lamp with a green metal shade hung from the rafters above. Waters had gotten interested in the orchard outside his door and was setting out to restore it. When I came to visit, I often found him at the table, poring over a catalog from Stark Brothers, the one that said "Stark Trees Bear Fruit" in white letters on the black silhouette of a bear. Sometimes he was looking through a copy of the *Farmer's Almanac*, or studying a book he had sent away for to learn about the apple trees and how to care for them. When he wasn't reading them, he kept the catalogs and books together on shelves above a little table next to the white-painted iron bedstead.

The east and west walls had windows that swung open at the bottom to let in fresh air, and Waters said he could see the sun rise and set through those windows. The only door was set in the south wall and led out onto a small porch with a little lean-to roof held up by posts on each side. Waters liked to sit out on the porch when the weather was good. From his hilltop, he could see across the valley below to the hills beyond. He could see a ways up the Glory Road to the east, see the creek flowing alongside it. To the west he had a view of the barn and part of Hal's house behind it.

Not long after we came to the ranch, Waters also signed up for weekly newspaper delivery. "Gotta keep up on the doin's in the world," he said. "Things happenin' all the time worth knowin' about. Newspaper be the best way to keep up with it all." The mail only came once a week, brought by a man named Sully who drove a Model T pickup. We were the only ones lived near to the end of the road, and so we were the last house on Sully's route. Waters looked out for the mail when it came, especially the newspaper. He was always waiting beside the mailbox when Sully showed up.

I never saw a man who took to the newspaper like Waters did. When the paper arrived, Waters would sit down at the table with it, spread the pages carefully on the green oilcloth, and read it from front to back. Sometimes he read it more than once. Sometimes he would cut articles out of the paper and paste them on the walls of his cabin. When I asked him about this, he told me, "The world full of strange people who do strange things to each other. I just like to keep track of the foolishness."

Waters said he started pasting newspapers on the wall 'cause it was cold in his cabin. The outside boards had been laid over the framing. The inside walls were unfinished. Over time the boards had shrunk a little, and wind whistled through the gaps. Pasting the newspapers over the gaps sealed them, making the cabin less drafty.

The passing weeks might just as well have been measured by those clippings on the cabin wall. Waters spent several weeks' collecting paste-worthy items, arranging them on the table till he got them the way he wanted. I watched him make his paste with flour and water. He mixed it in a pan with a spoon till it was about as thick as pancake batter. Then he cooked it on the stove till it just started to bubble and set it aside to cool. When it was done, he showed me how to brush on the paste while he put the articles up on the wall.

Even when I wasn't there to help, Waters kept cutting

out articles from the paper and pasting them over the ones already there, and eventually all the inside walls of the cabin were covered with newspaper. After a while he started organizing the clippings. One wall had newspaper articles about world affairs, wars and the like; one was about people and the strange things they did; each wall had a different purpose. Every time I saw them, the walls were different.

Like Waters, I wanted to know what was going on in the world, too, but I found my own way of doing it. On the back of a magazine, I found an advertisement for a crystal set. "Build your own crystal radio!" It said. I badgered Uncle Hal until he gave me enough money to send away for a kit to build the radio. He made me pay it back by doing chores around the house, but it was worth it. I waited and waited, stood by our mailbox like Waters did, hoping that the crystal set would come. When it finally did, I spent two weeks making it, using a Quick Quaker Oats box with Ben Franklin on the front, winding the coil around the box and mounting the whole thing on a board. I found some wire in the barn that was left over from building the house. Waters helped me string the wire under the eaves of the roof from one end of the house to the other. When it was finished, we ran a lead from the antenna through my bedroom window to the crystal set. And it worked!

Late at night, especially, I could hear programs from all over. I liked to listen to shows like *Gangbusters* and a new show called the *Green Hornet*. With his manservant Kato, Britt Reid was a newspaper publisher by day and a vigilante by night. I really liked *Amos 'n Andy*, too, but Waters didn't think much of them, said it was funny how the only Negroes on the radio were two white men.

Waters was mostly interested in the news. He told me about Father Divine and his "heavens" in Harlem and other cities, told how Hitler wouldn't present Jesse Owens with the medal he won, said he thought Roosevelt was sure to beat Landon in November. News programs let us know what was going on in the world. Boulder Dam was making electricity, and dead presidents were looking out from Mount Rushmore. But it all seemed as far away to me as the civil war in Spain. The newsmen called it the Depression, said lots of folks all over the country were out of work. Some stood in long lines to get handouts, or look for jobs, they said. There was no news about Momma.

I asked Uncle Hal once about leaving the mill so suddenly. What about his job there? Wouldn't people be mad about his leaving like that? He said he wasn't worried about that, said folks that worked there didn't really know much about what went on there. He said orders had fallen off to the point where the mill would probably only last a few more months at best. One of the owners had "seen the handwriting on the wall," he said, and had run off with a lot of money. That and the drop in orders would be the end of it.

Uncle Hal didn't talk much about his plans for the ranch, about his dead wife and all. I only knew about that from what Momma had said. He just said, "It's good to have land. Man that has land won't starve to death. He can fish or hunt, plant something in the ground, raise livestock. He might work himself to death, but he won't starve."

6

Thinking about Daddy still made me cry, and my worries about Momma colored my dreams, but every day dawned without them beside me. I woke up in this cold little room that Momma said I could "grow into" and make my own. I thought it would take a long time for that to happen with only Uncle Hal and Waters for company.

Uncle Hal wasn't like most of the men who worked at the mill and spent their wages on drink and Saturday night fun. He was a thrifty man who didn't waste his money on foolishness. He had made good money as the foreman at the mill, and he had enough set aside to get started on the ranch.

"Orla and I had plans for this place," he told me once. "But after she was gone, I just lost interest in it. Went off to do other things for a while. But it could still turn into something with a little work. We'll get by until then. You'll see."

Not long after that, he used some of his savings to buy himself a horse. It was a big horse—sixteen hands, Uncle Hal said—taller than most. He called the horse Shorty, like some big fellas are called Tiny, but he was short-tempered as well. Scariest horse I was ever around. He had gray eyes that looked right through you. Waters said those eyes were a sure sign that horse was mean, and neither of us would go near him. But Uncle Hal had a way with animals.

When he first brought Shorty home, he was skittish and balky and hard to handle, even for Hal. One day he planted his feet and refused to budge when Hal tried to ride him. When Hal kicked in with his heels to make him go, Shorty snorted and arched his back and tried to toss

Uncle Hal out of the saddle, but Hal just held on till Shorty stopped bucking. Then he got down from the saddle, held on to the reins, and walked up to where he could look Shorty in the eye. The two of them just stared at each other. Shorty flattened his ears and gave Hal that wild-eyed, mean-looking stare of his. But Hal just stood his ground and stared right back at him. After a few minutes of that, Hal whacked Shorty on his forehead with the end of his bullwhip. Then he pulled on the bridle and brought Shorty's face up close to his own. He looked Shorty in the eye for a bit longer, and then stroked the side of his head for a long time. Shorty never gave him any trouble after that. In fact, I think that horse came to love Hal in a way Waters and I could never understand.

Hal liked to hunt and fish. In the beginning he *needed* to hunt and fish. We didn't have anything to eat; the renter Hal had sent away had planted a garden, but there wasn't much left of it in the fall when we got to the ranch. Waters' old, overgrown apple trees had a few apples on them, but we didn't have much else at first. So Waters and I fished the creek, and Hal hunted.

Waters had found some cane poles Uncle Hal had left in the barn when he went away the first time, and we used those when we went fishing. The Glory Road pretty much followed a creek that came down from back in the hills somewhere. Occasionally the valley widened out a bit, and the creek meandered through the open country, taking its own sweet time on its way to Glory. Then the road veered away from the creek, looking to shorten the distance to town by taking a straighter route, but the creek was never very far from the road. Waters and I had followed the road up the creek, stepping off once in a while to go down to the creek and look for a good spot to fish. After a lot of looking, we found a spot that became one of our favorites. It was a big hole in a bend of the creek where the willows and redbud didn't crowd the edge of the river. The stump of a big redwood lay along one edge of the pool, and some alders had sprouted from the top of the stump, making a leafy canopy that shaded the pool, but didn't hang low enough to get in the way when we tried to toss a line in the water. Just upstream from the stump, the creek narrowed and the water rippled over the rocks as it flowed into the big pool.

The trouble with cane pole fishing is that the pole has to be long enough to reach out far enough so you can flip your line in the water without getting tangled in bushes or trees. And then, if you get a nibble, you have to be able to flip your fish up on the bank before it wiggles free of the hook. The spot we picked was a good one, no trees hanging down to the water's edge and a nice sandy bank just past the downstream end of the stump.

When Waters went fishing, there was a lot of ritual involved. He carried an old Velvet tobacco tin in his pocket, which he filled with whole kernel corn or little bits of cheese that he called chum. He used this to attract the fish by sprinkling a little on the water. He went upstream to the spot where the creek narrowed and rippled over the rocks and tossed a little chum into the water, so it would drift down into the hole and attract the fish. He also used to rub some smelly stuff he called "asafidity" on his line, which was also supposed to attract the fish.

I was a worm man, myself. Since Uncle Hal got Shorty, we had a ready supply of horse manure, which got shoveled out of the barn into a pile in back. That pile was a gold mine as far as worms were concerned. I dug around in the bottom of the pile with a shovel, and in no time I had all the worms I needed. I popped them into an old Hills Brothers Coffee can

I found in the barn, and I was set to go. I wasn't interested in all Waters' hocus-pocus stuff, with his talk about how "you gotta hold your nose just right" and other nonsense. I just put a nice worm on the hook and let it do its job. Seemed to me one way was just about as good as the other, 'cause sometimes he'd catch more, and the next time I'd do better. And sometimes both of us got skunked. I think that's just the nature of fishing.

Anyway, our favorite hole was easier to fish than most of the brushy, overgrown stretches, and we usually went there first before moving on to the more challenging spots along the creek. We usually caught a few fish, enough to fill a good-sized frying pan, but we always hoped for something a little bigger. There was a big cutthroat trout in that hole when we first started fishing there. We saw him sometimes just cruising around the hole, occasionally rising to the surface to take a bug that had the misfortune to fall into the water and was struggling and kicking itself around on top. We tried to catch him on several occasions, but he never took the bait. We tried to toss the line out just right, the baited hook making a soft landing right near the big guy, but he just looked at it and swam on. We got to where we had a lot of respect for that fish. We figured he hadn't got that big by being stupid, and after a while we took to calling him Solomon, 'cause he'd outsmarted us so many times.

Uncle Hal took me deer hunting with him a few times. I supposed he thought it would give me something to do. Maybe he wanted to teach me about the things he knew. I'm not sure how much I learned about hunting, but our first hunting trip gave me a look at a side of Hal I hadn't seen before.

We had set out early in the morning, following a path

that led up into the hills behind Waters' cabin. It was cold and foggy, and water dripped from the trees at either side of the path. When we reached the top of the nearest hill, we could see an opening beyond a stand of trees in front of us. Uncle Hal held his finger to his lips, then bent and whispered in my ear. "We'll spread out a little and walk through those trees, maybe drive something out into the open." We moved twenty or thirty feet apart, then started into the trees.

After we had walked a ways into the woods, we heard a scrambling rustle among the leaves, and then the thump of hoofbeats running ahead of us. We just kept on walking through the underbrush and the trees until we could see into the opening ahead of us. Standing about fifty yards out in the open were three deer, a doe and two yearlings. They stood, ears up, looking back at us. Behind them, a little further out, was a big buck. The doe turned and began to walk away from us. The buck turned and began to run toward the other side of the clearing. Hal shouldered his rifle and took a quick shot, missing the buck. It bounded away then, leaping as it ran toward the edge of the clearing. Hal took another shot, and the buck stiffened as the bullet caught him in midair, but he recovered when he landed and trotted away toward the edge of the clearing where the land dropped away sharply.

Uncle Hal and I followed right away, running to the edge of the clearing where we could see down into the canyon below. The deer was down at the bottom of the ravine. We could hear it crashing through the brush below us.

"Sit down, Justin," Hal said.

"What do you mean? Are we just going to let him go?"

"Don't worry about that deer. He isn't going very far. A gutshot deer that's panicked will run a long ways. Best not to chase him. He'll get sick and want to lay down. We'll just wait."

The bottom of the ravine was a long way down. The sides were steep, and I didn't see any path to the bottom. "How are we going to get him out of there? If we find him, I mean. It's a hard climb in and out of there."

"It'll be all right. You just sit here. I'm gonna go get Shorty." And then he turned around and started walking back the way we had come.

I watched Uncle Hal walk back along the path until he went over the hill and out of sight. Then I sat down to wait.

About half an hour later, Uncle Hal and Shorty topped the rise and started down the hill toward me. When they got to me, they stopped. Hal got down, stroked Shorty's cheek, and looked at me. "Shorty and I are gonna go get that buck. Just wait here and watch, understand?"

"Sure," I said, even though I didn't understand how he expected to get down to that deer, much less bring it out of that canyon.

Uncle Hal mounted up, and they started down into the trees below me. When they got down a ways, they stopped for a minute or so, Uncle Hal looking around before he urged Shorty forward into the trees and down into the canyon. They disappeared from sight quickly, but I could follow their progress pretty well by listening to the sound of Shorty moving through the underbrush. After a while, though, I couldn't see or hear them. I sat down on a rock at the edge of the ravine and waited.

An hour or more had passed when I thought I heard something and looked down into the canyon. I couldn't see anything, but every once in a while I thought I heard something down there. A little while later, I heard it again. It was Shorty, panting and blowing. Hal was stopping to rest Shorty as they climbed the hill. When they stopped, I could hear him blow, kind of like the sound you make when you put your lips together loosely and force air through them.

Then I heard them clearly, coming up through the brush and trees, heard them stop to rest, heard Hal talking to that horse, coaxing him along in a low voice. There was respect in his tone. I could hear how he loved that horse, could tell he cared about how hard Shorty was working.

I was astonished when I finally caught sight of them. Coming over a little rise and into view for the first time, Hal stopped to rest Shorty before starting the final climb out of the canyon. Hal was mounted on Shorty, the deer draped over his flanks, tied on behind the saddle. Shorty blew steam from his nose and mouth. His withers and chest were covered in foam—thick, foamy sweat that slid down his legs as he stood there. The sight nearly took my breath away. I'd heard stories about animals giving their all for a person, but I had never seen anything like that before, nor have I seen anything to equal it since. I realized then what I was seeing. That horse would do anything for Hal—or die trying.

Eventually Uncle Hal and Shorty climbed to the top of the last rise, and Hal dismounted. He looked Shorty in the eye, stroked his cheek, and talked to him a while. I watched them without saying anything. Something remarkable had happened between them, and I felt like an outsider. We all rested for a while, and then we walked back over the hill and down to the house. Hal and I walked on either side of Shorty, who still carried the deer strapped to his back.

When we got back to the barn, we hung the deer from one of the roof beams, and Hal dressed it, gutting and skinning it efficiently. He left it hanging to cure, covering it with a burlap sack to keep off the flies. When he was finished, he wiped Shorty down, washed the sweat away, dried him off, and rubbed him down. He fed and watered Shorty and sat with him while he ate and drank. He was still sitting with him when I left and returned to the house.

7

When fall came and the leaves fell from the trees, Waters began working on the old orchard in the field outside his cabin. The trees were old and overgrown. "Trees got a life just like folks do," Waters said. "But they live longer when someone take care of them. Nobody been looking after these for a long time now. Be some work to it, but most of them will come back." He set out to save what he could.

He started by cutting away the dead wood, dragging it away and piling it up for burning in the winter. After that was done, he "studied the bones of each tree," he said, and tried to tell "which way it wanted to grow." He talked about the trees as if they were people who needed his help. He saw where the limbs crossed over each other, studied the spots where they had rubbed together, and cut them back to reveal the tree's true "character," as he called it.

He knew all the trees' names, he said. He had looked at the apples that were on the trees when we got to the ranch, had looked in the catalogs and the books he had bought, and he had identified the trees by looking at the pictures in the books and reading the descriptions printed there.

One day, I saw him standing by one of his trees when I came up the hill toward his cabin. When I caught up to him, I asked him what he was doing.

"I was just studying this tree. It's a crabapple. Not much for fruit but interesting anyway. Want to know why?"

I didn't particularly want to know about his tree, but I said, "Why?" Out of politeness.

"Well, there weren't any real apple trees in America

before the Europeans came. There were some crabapples that were native to America, little scrawny ones that the Indians knew about. Didn't produce very good apples, but they were real sturdy and had great roots. Kind of like the Indians.

"Then people started coming from other countries. Some of them brought seeds and planted trees. Some of them grafted their trees' branches onto the sturdy roots of those crabapples. All kinds of apple trees from all sorts of places. Pretty soon America got all kinds of apples grafted onto sturdy stock. New kinds of apples began to be created right here. The sons and daughters, let's just say, of those first apple trees, are making new trees—American trees—different from what they came from, but even better than the ones that came before."

Waters walked me down the rows of trees in the old orchard. "Look at this fellow here. This one's an Astrachan, brought over from Russia about a hundred years ago." He pointed to another tree across the row from the first. "And this one's a Gravenstein, brought over from Italy before 1800. And down there—he pointed to indicate one of the taller trees—"that one's called Northern Spy! What a great name for a tree!"

Waters and I walked together between the rows of trees. He pointed out different trees to me, told me their names and their history. They were Jonathan and Red June, Wealthy, and McIntosh, which Waters said came from Canada. There were Baldwins, which Waters said made good cider, and an apple called Winter Banana, and one called Seek-No-Further, which, I think, was my favorite name of all.

"You see, Justin? The apples are just like us. We started out with the Indians. We didn't think much of 'em, didn't treat 'em well, didn't understand their importance, just like those little crabapples. Then other people came, added what they were, who they were to the mix.

"Some of 'em came unwillingly, brought here 'gainst their will, some of them were forced out of their homes by hard times, by famine and the like, and some came just to see what this country was like. But altogether, they became something new, something different from what they were back where they came from, do y'see?"

"But they're all just apples, aren't they?'

"Sure. And we all just people. One the same as the rest. But sometimes people forget that, and put labels on each other and try to make one out to be better than another.

"I had an idea come to me when I was studying that crabapple tree over there. Don't you know you can graft limbs from one tree onto another?"

I did know that. I had seen it explained in one of Waters' books. You could take a branch from one tree—Waters called them scions—and graft it onto a tree of a different kind. There were pictures in his books that showed how it was done.

"Well that's what I aim to do. I'm gonna take slips from a whole bunch of these trees and see can I graft them to that old crabapple. I'm gonna make us a new tree, and I'm gonna call it the All-American."

Waters and I gathered scions from this year's growth on the old trees. He carefully labeled them and tied them into bundles and then wrapped them in moss that he had gathered. He placed the moss-wrapped bundles into a wooden frame that he had made and placed it under the edge of the porch outside his cabin.

"I'll check on 'em from time to time, make sure they don't dry out. Then when spring come, we'll see can we graft 'em onto that old crabapple tree."

8

November third rolled around, and Roosevelt beat the pants off Alf Landon, winning every state but Maine and Vermont. Waters was happier than a fiddler with a new tune. When the newspaper came, he added a whole new section to the news wall devoted to the election.

About the middle of November, it began to rain. The days were shorter, and winter was just around the corner. It hardly ever snowed, Uncle Hal said, but it sure did rain. Sometimes it rained so hard he said it was "raining pitchforks and hammer handles," which made about as much sense as when people said it rained cats and dogs. I mostly stayed in the house when the weather was like that, but whenever the firewood stacked on the front porch started to run low, Uncle Hal sent me out to the woodshed to bring in some more. The wheelbarrow Hal kept in the woodshed had open sides and a flat front that angled up to keep the wood from falling off. The spoked wheel was metal with a narrow tread. When the ground was soaked from the rain, that metal wheel sank in and made balancing the loaded wheelbarrow a real challenge. More than once, it had tipped over and pulled me ass end over teakettle with it. I spouted a few choice words I'd heard the millhands use while I was gathering up the firewood that had spilled in the muddy yard. Uncle Hal usually said, "Oh, pshaw" when he bollixed something or other. He was the only one I ever knew who said that. For a man who carried a bullwhip, he wasn't much for cussing.

Once in a while, when I got tired of sitting in the house, just watching the rain come down, I threw on a jacket and one of Hal's old hats that hung on a peg in the hurling room and ran down the road to the barn. I liked the way the barn smelled of hay and manure, of unpainted wood and cedar shingles. I slid open the big barn door just wide enough to squeeze in, and then since it was dark inside with the door almost closed, I usually took down one of the kerosene lanterns that hung on the wall and lit it with a match from the red, white, and blue box of Diamond Safety Matches Uncle Hal kept dry in a jar on the shelf below the lanterns. Then I made my way over to where the Model A was parked. I put the lantern on the workbench below the only window in the wall, its dirty panes smothered in spider webs and years of grime that blocked most of the light. Then I opened the car door, climbed up on the running board, and slid in under the steering wheel. I sat there, pretended I was driving, thinking about how Daddy and Waters had pooled their money to buy the car, and about how Hal had used it to get Waters and Momma and me out of that pickle back at the mill. And I thought about how he had used it to take Momma away from here.

Sometimes I sat in the back and remembered Daddy driving Momma and me to see that carnival, his rough hands resting loosely on the wheel. I remembered the Sunday drives and riding somewhere for a picnic with the hamper on the seat between Waters and me. I wondered more than once where Hal had taken Momma. He had been gone overnight, didn't come back till later the next day. She was somewhere far away, I knew for sure.

Sometimes I just stayed in the house and watched the weather outside. Uncle Hal had a piano he had bought for Orla. "There was a woman loved music," Hal said, "Always singing or humming when she worked. Could play anything she put her mind to." She had loved music, and he bought the piano so she would feel more at home. It was in the front room, a player piano, a big ebony upright model. Orla could play on her own, Hal said, but he had bought the player piano anyway. It came with a cabinet full of music rolls, and it seemed like he was getting more for his money.

When he left after Orla's death, he had rented the ranch out to a single man who had stayed on the hill in the cabin where Waters lived now, and the house was closed up tight. Orla was the last one to play the piano, and for the longest time Uncle Hal wouldn't let me touch it. Sometimes he would sit in the front parlor by the fireplace and just look across the room at the piano, remembering, I suppose. There was sheet music still on the stand, just the way she had left it. It was one of the few things left to remind him of her.

One night, after he had sat in the room by the fire a little longer than usual, nursing a drink or two, he called me into the room and told me I could play the piano if I wanted to.

"When Orla played, this little house just swelled with the music she made, seemed bigger somehow. Won't be the same, but it might be nice to hear music in the house anyway." I was so excited about playing the piano, I didn't realize till I thought about it later how sad and quiet he seemed.

He took a long time explaining to me how the piano worked. He wanted, I thought, to make sure I would take care of it and not break anything, but later I thought there must have been more to his gentle manner than that. His attitude toward me had seemed to soften—just for a moment—but I felt a change. He took the sheet music down from the stand, lifted the seat on the bench, and carefully placed it inside with the others already there. He showed me the two doors in the middle above the keyboard that slid apart. Inside was where the music roll went. He showed me how the roll fit between two ends that stuck out on the top part, and how to pull the paper down from the top and hook it onto the roller at the bottom.

Then he showed me the two big pedals on the floor. He told me how pushing the pedals built up the air pressure that would make the piano play. I sat down on the piano bench and started pushing on those pedals with my feet–left, right, left, right. I could feel the air pressure build up against the pedals, and the paper roll began to scroll down and wrap itself around the roller at the bottom. Then the words appeared on the music roll, and the holes that were punched into the paper made the music play. As the music started, the air whooshed out, and I had to pedal faster to keep the pressure up. When I got to the end of the song, the paper came loose from the top roll and went flap-flap-flapping around the bottom roller.

I wanted to play all the rolls that were in the cabinet, but Uncle Hal only let me play two songs before he asked me to play one called The *Rose of Tralee*. Orla had liked that song, he said, and hearing it again reminded him of her. I pumped the pedals, and the words scrolled down:

"She was lovely and fair as the rose of the summer
Yet, 'twas not her beauty alone that won me.
Oh no! 'twas the truth in her eye ever beaming
That made me love Mary, the Rose of Tralee."

That was the first time Uncle Hal ever let me play the piano, but it would not be the last. As time went by I sometimes asked to play the piano in the evenings, usually when I was restless and couldn't figure out anything else to do. It was just an entertainment to me, but I knew it was something more to Uncle Hal. On those occasions when he let me play, I could choose two rolls to play, but I always had to end with his request for the *Rose of Tralee*.

At other times when there wasn't much to do, I thought about Fuzzy and Miss Gravy and Dora and Dottie, and wondered what would happen to them if the mill closed like Uncle Hal said it would. Miss Gravy would find a place for herself, I supposed, but what about Fuzzy and the girls? Where would they go? Maybe they were gone already, gone to some other far-off place like we had. Maybe they were in some big city, standing in one of those breadlines I heard about in the news. Or would they end up like me, in a place like this, without any friends to play with, not knowing where their parents had gone?

9

There was nothing much to celebrate at Thanksgiving, though we did have a nice dinner of venison, roasted till it fell apart, with onions and gravy. Uncle Hal was a fair cook when he wanted to be, which wasn't very often. Waters never ate dinner at the house, but I kept badgering Uncle Hal until he gave in and let me invite him to eat Thanksgiving dinner with us.

It was funny how those two acted around each other. I could be with either of them, and everything would be fine. Hal wasn't much for talking, but he would show me how to do things—how to sharpen a knife or an axe, how to track a deer, how to mend a fence, or how to split firewood and stack it properly. Waters talked about anything and everything. There didn't seem to be any limits on what we talked about. We talked about what he read in the paper, what I heard on the radio. He talked about his apples and about things he read in his books. He talked to me about me, sometimes—asked me how I was—and acted like he really wanted to know.

But Uncle Hal and Waters hardly ever talked to each other about anything. They pretty much kept to themselves. There was something between them, and I didn't understand what it was, but I could feel it just the same. Whatever it was, it was always there. Whenever they did talk to each other, they were like neighbors talking over the back fence. They talked about the weather, about things that needed to be done around the ranch, but then they went their separate ways. The one thing they never talked about, at least around me, was Momma. I asked Hal about her sometimes, but he just ignored me or, more often, changed the subject to something he was more comfortable with.

"Hal just want to protect your Momma," Waters said. "He worried that those men lose their jobs at the mill and come looking for trouble. Might be he's right about that. I don't know. He got her in a safe place, I know that much for sure. We just have to wait and see what happen."

Waters always acted like he didn't know any more than I did, and the conversation sort of died away after a little while.

I hadn't expected anything special from either Hal or Waters at Christmas. Momma always got Daddy to cut a little tree, and we decorated it with paper chains we made from colored paper and popcorn garlands we strung together. On Christmas Eve, she always read me "A Visit from St. Nicholas," and sang one of her Irish Christmas songs. I remembered the one that said, "The prettiest picture you've ever seen is Christmas in Killarney with all of the folks at home." It made me want to cry if I thought about it too long. Christmas in Cooper's Gulch wasn't much, but we were all together then. It was all so different now.

But our Christmas on the Glory Road was all right. Uncle Hal gave me a pair of boots he had sent away for. Later he showed me how I could warm the boots in the oven and then rub Huberd's Shoe Grease on each one to make the boots waterproof. Waters gave me a wooden train set he had carved himself. It had a locomotive and three log cars. He had stained the engine black with shoe polish and made little logs for the cars from branches he had cut from his apple trees. The log cars hooked together with little pegs that fit in holes at the ends of the cars, and he had made the cars so that the log platforms would tip to dump the logs.

"I recollect how you pestered your daddy to let you watch them dump the logs when you just a little boy–sat on Billy's shoulders and laughed at the big splash they made. Even when you got too big to lift, you always stood with Billy when they unloaded."

I thought I was a little too old for toys like that, but I could see he cared some for me by the time he had put into making it, and I thanked him for it. I told him it would remind me of our time in Cooper's Gulch, and I would put it on the shelf in the bedroom where I could look at it whenever I wanted to. I couldn't really say out loud how much it meant to me. It made me happy and sad at the same time. It was a gift from his heart to mine. I knew that for certain.

I liked their gifts, probably even more because I hadn't expected to get them, but it wasn't the same as the other Christmases I had known. I guessed it wouldn't ever be like that again. I didn't have any gifts for them, but I made them Christmas cards. I pasted pictures I found in some old magazines out in the barn onto colored paper. Uncle Hal's was a picture of a man on a horse riding on a trail through the woods. Waters' card had a picture of an apple tree.

I had cut out little circles and colored them with crayons and pasted them on the tree to show different kinds of apples all growing on the same tree. Inside each card I wrote "Merry Christmas. Love, Justin."

10

After months of cold and rain, spring finally arrived. March downpours faded away into April showers. Winter had lost its punch, and the days grew longer. Even though we still got an occasional shower, the weather warmed and the gentle rains did little to dampen our spirits. The creek stayed in its banks. The water cleared and lost its muddy look. Finally what we pumped from the creek began to look like water again, losing its coffee-with-cream color. The hills turned green, and the redbud began to bloom, a sure sign, Waters said, that spring was here. He said it would soon be time to graft the shoots onto his apple tree.

Waters had cut back the limbs on the old crabapple in the winter when the tree was bare. He said the tree was pretty old, and so we were only going to put grafts on the top and center part. The rest would have to wait another year. He had cut away the dead wood and the limbs that rubbed against each other, just like on the other trees. He cut the limbs he wanted to graft off closer to the main trunk of the tree. Then he split the end of each limb. He took the scions, trimmed them off on one end so they had only three buds on them, then used his pocketknife to carve the other end into a wedge shape. He took two of the scions and carefully pushed them into the outside edges of the split he had made in the end of the tree limb, making sure the inner bark of the limb and the scion were touching. Then he covered the whole joint with some black, tarry-looking stuff he had in a can.

After I had watched him for a while, he let me trim

the scions and carve the ends into wedge shapes. Then he would do the grafting. After each graft, he would tie a label on the limb saying what kind of apple it was. I asked him how long it would take to see the new apples.

"You gonna have to wait a while—couple of years, probably. Some of the grafts won't take. That's why we put two on each limb. The ones that do grow will take a while. Next year we'll do some more grafts on the other branches. Be lots of different kinds of apples on this tree one day."

"Seems like a long time to wait to see a tree grow apples."

"Well, it's like I said. Took a long time to get all those different kinds of apples to grow in this country, all the different types of people, too. This the 'All-American.' We just got to wait and see what it look like when it's done."

Waters had plenty to do with his apples. The older trees in the orchard apparently took to being pruned. Pretty soon they burst into bloom, and the trees were covered in pink and white blossoms. He started talking about what he would do when the apples came on.

"We need an apple house—a place to store the apples, keep 'em cool, so they last longer. A place where I can make cider and store it for a while."

"How you planning on doing that?" I said.

"I got an idea—been reading up on it. You can help me if you want, 'less you too busy to bother."

I wasn't too busy, of course. Most of the time I had nothing to do 'cept chores, and they didn't usually take too long. Waters explained that we needed to find a cool place where we could store the apples so they wouldn't rot so soon. There was no place like that we could use, so we would have to make our own. He got his idea from a book he had read.

He said we could make a dugout in the hillside below his cabin. We would dig into the hill, make a flat floor, and cut three straight sides in the dirt for the side and back walls. Then we would shore up the dirt walls with wood or stone, build a front wall to close it in, and make a roof over the whole thing. It sounded easy when he explained it.

I soon found out that digging is hard work, even in the springtime when the ground is soft. Dirt is happy where it is and won't give up its grip just 'cause you want it somewhere else. I tried to help, but Waters did most all the work. I would stick with it for a while, then find some excuse to leave him on his own. Waters somehow managed to make hard work look easy. He was strong like Daddy was, but there was a rhythm and grace in his movements that I wished I could manage. All my efforts seemed ham-fisted compared with his. When the work was hard, I always ended up red-faced and sweaty, but Waters looked like he was enjoying himself.

"Give it a little time yet, Justin," he told me. "You just young, got to grow a little while longer 'til you come into your own. A man got work to do going to find the strength to do it and feel the joy it bring."

It took us (mostly him, actually) the better part of a month just to dig out all that dirt and haul it off, but eventually the hole got dug, and we started on the walls. We hauled stones from the creek and stacked them on the sides of the hole we had dug. Waters laid the stones and made some mortar to hold them together, but it was pretty slow going. I mostly went with him to the creek to pick out stones and helped load them onto the big flat wheelbarrow we usually used down at the house to haul wood from the woodshed to the porch. When the rocks were loaded on the wheelbarrow, it was too heavy for me to lift and push, so Waters did all the real work.

After we had lined the hole and Waters mortared the stones together, we built another wall at the front of the apple house with two rows of stones and built a door in it. Finally, we went into the woods where some smaller redwoods grew. Waters picked out a tree and chopped it down. Then he peeled the bark from the tree and hauled the bark down the hill to his cabin. He chopped up the bark, and we packed it into the space between the stone walls and the dirt and into the spaces between the rows of stones in the front wall. All of this would help keep it cool inside, Waters said. Finally, Waters and I went back to the redwood tree he had chopped down. He had brought a long saw with a handle at each end.

"This here's called a 'misery whip', and in about ten minutes, you'll know why. Grab a-hold of that end."

I took the other end of the saw, and we walked over to the log. He stood on one side of the log, and I stood on the other.

"The idea here is to pull the saw back and forth—not push it. I'll pull it one way. Then you pull it back. Understand?"

I held on while Waters pulled back on the end of the saw. When he stopped, I tried to pull it back, but it didn't want to move.

"Don't pull down on the saw. Just make it slide back. Let the saw do the work."

Waters always made work look easy. He had rolled the sleeves on his old chambray shirt, and I could see the muscles work under his smooth brown forearms. His concentration showed in his face, but he never appeared to strain himself at all. His movements were smooth and sure, and always there was that ease that I wished I could command.

Somehow I managed to drag the saw back, but it was still hard. Waters seemed to be doing most of the work, as usual, but eventually the log parted. After that we rested for a bit before making another cut.

"This here's our story pole," he said, pointing to a long pole we had brought with us. "See the marks I made along the pole? Measured those out with my foot, marked them with my pocketknife. Now we know how many 'feet' long to make those logs, so they all be the same."

He laughed when he said that, and I laughed with him, but he said that was how people did things back when they didn't have proper tools. He said a grownup man's hand was about nine inches from the tip of the thumb to the tip of the little finger, that that was called a "span", another useful measurement 'cause you always had your hands with you wherever you went.

Later, we cut the log to the length Waters wanted for the roof beams. When the log was cut into lengths, Waters used a sledge and wedges to split the log into thick slabs. We dragged these back to the cabin and down to the apple house, where we slid them into place on top of the walls, fixing them so that they sloped down and hung over the front wall. Nothing ever seemed to get thrown away on the ranch, and Waters had found some sheets of corrugated tin roofing out behind the barn. They were rusty, but good enough to use. Waters and I hauled them up the hill and nailed them on top of the slabs on the roof.

It had taken a long time, but Waters had his apple house. Now all he needed was the apples to put in it.

11

The old Model A sat in the barn most of the time. Occasionally Waters would start it up–to keep the battery charged, he said. And once in a while Uncle Hal would drive it to Glory to pick up feed for Shorty or groceries when we were running low. I saw the town for the first time on one of those trips.

The Glory Road turned into Main Street as we came into town. There were a few houses on either side of the street before you came to the main buildings, and there was one little side street, more like an alley, that crossed Main. On the left side was a gas station with two yellow Shell gas pumps on an island under the roof that poked out from the office building. In the back was a garage with several open stalls. A few cars in various stages of repair peeked out of the open doors.

On the corner across from the gas station, two rough-looking customers stood outside a barroom called the Snug. It was about the ugliest building I'd seen so far in Glory. It was old like some of the other buildings in town, but it was really run-down looking. The lower floor windows had been painted over so you couldn't see in, and a sign hanging over the door between them said, "The Snug" and had a picture of a beer mug underneath the name. Upstairs, some of the windows were broken and boarded up. One had a piece of cardboard stuck in the frame. A brown stain streaked down one wall from a rusted drainpipe. Hal said the building hadn't seen a coat of paint "since Hector was a pup."

Hal pulled up in front of the gas pumps. An older

man in grease-stained overalls came through the office and stepped out, wiping his hands on a red rag.

"He'p you?" He inquired, stuffing the rag into one of his back pockets.

"Fill it up, Al. Should take about eight gallons," Hal said.

Al took off the gas cap on the dash in front of the Model A's windshield and turned to the old-fashioned gas pump. He took up the hose and put the nozzle into the gas tank. Then he pumped the handle up and down. Gasoline flowed into the glass at the top of the pump under the big white clam shell. When it hit the eight gallon mark, Al stopped pumping. Then he squeezed the handle on the nozzle and the gas ran down from the pump into the tank. When he had filled the tank, he hung the nozzle back on the pump and replaced the cap on the car, pulling the red rag out of his pocket and carefully wiping around the cap.

"Be eighty cents."

"Thanks, Al," Hal said, handing him a dollar.

Al fished in his overall pocket, came up with two dimes, handed them to Hal. "See you next time," he said. He turned and walked back through the office door, stuffing the rag back in his pocket and heading toward the garage out back.

Hal started the car, and we headed down the street, passing between two rows of buildings, most of them stores, some with living quarters upstairs. One of them was a Rexall drug store with an orange and blue sign above the windows that said "Babcock's Rexall Drugs." There was another door to the side of the store entrance. It had a sign that read "Rooms to Let" with a painted hand pointing up.

There was a feed store –"McManus Feed and Seed," according to the sign that hung across the loading dock beside the store–that sold tack and supplies for livestock, hay and grain– stuff like that. Two men in overalls and flat caps were tossing sacks of grain onto the back of a flatbed truck as we passed by. On the opposite side of the street was the Bon Ton Cafe, with a sign in the window that said they were serving breakfast and lunch. Hal tried to make a joke about getting chicken feed on one side of the street and feeding on chicken on the other side, but I didn't think it was too funny. Hal drove up the street to Sadler's market, a grocery store with a post office in the back. The storefront was green with a row of black tiles under the large picture window. There were windows in the second story above the store, and lace curtains waved in one that was open a few inches. Weekly specials painted in red and blue on white butcher paper covered most of the store window. A bald man in a white shirt with a long green apron was sweeping the sidewalk in front of the door when Hal parked at the curb in one of the angled parking spaces.

When I opened the door, Hal said, "Just wait by the car. Don't go wandering off," and he went into the store. After he went in, I sat on the running board for a bit till I got bored. Finally I got up and walked up the street a ways. Glory boasted one real intersection, a cross street that went off to ranch country on either side of town. There was a stop sign there, but it looked like it would be a long time before they would need to brag about having their own traffic light. The Glory Road continued straight ahead of me. It went past a few more houses, then headed out toward the hills in the distance, where it disappeared from view. I took a look up and down the side road. There wasn't much to look at either way, just a couple of houses with big trees in the front yards up the street on the left. On the right side there was a one-story building that had a picture window in front and a door to the side that had "Sheriff" in black letters outlined in gold on its window. There were a few cars parked on the street, most of them looking like they'd known hard times, just like their owners probably had. Across from the Sheriff's office, but further down the street, there was a bigger white building with broad wooden steps leading up to a covered porch over the double doors. It had a little tower on the side with a bell hanging in it near the top. It looked like a church, but when I crossed the street and went to take a look, I noticed a sign on the front wall that said "Glory Community Church and School." Beyond that I could see a few more houses, and then the road made a turn and I couldn't see any further.

I figured Hal had probably finished his business at the store by now, and I was about to hightail it back when I saw a boy about my age walking toward me.

"You live around here?" I asked.

"Yeah," he said, "On the other side of Main Street, in that green house with the picket fence."

I had seen the house when I was looking around earlier. "The sign there says it's a church and a school. If it's a school, how come no kids are there?"

"Ain't no school right now. Got no teacher. Last one got married. Run off to the big city. Probably glad to get outta here. Ain't nothin' much to keep a teacher here. School's supposed to open again if we get another. Maybe they find someone by next year."

"How many kids go there?"

"'Bout twelve—fifteen, maybe. It's just one teacher in a room with all of us. Couple little kids, some ones too old to be in school, but the teacher lets 'em if they want to come. Kids come from all around when there's school."

"What's your name? Mine's Justin. People call me Just."

"I'm Wiley Travers. You new here?"

"Been here a while. But we live way out on the Glory Road. Maybe I'll see you again sometime. Say, I better be going, or my Uncle will have my hide. He's just down at the store getting some groceries. See you around." I started running down the street to the store.

"Right," Wiley called after me. "Come by the house. Ain't hardly no kids around here."

When I got back to the store, Hal was standing outside, talking to the fellow in the green apron. The grocery man stood in the doorway, saying something I couldn't hear, leaning in closer to Hal when he spoke. Then both of them broke out laughing.

"That's a good one," Hal said, still chuckling. I was glad they were having a good time.

Maybe he wouldn't be mad at me for running off. Come to think of it, that was about the only time I ever heard him laugh. Most of the time he was serious with me, and especially with Waters.

When he finally saw me, Uncle Hal looked up and said, "Well, it's about time you showed up. I told you not to run off. We were about to organize a search party, weren't we, Mike?"

"Sure were—Glory's such a big place, easy to get lost and all." He laughed at his own joke, and then he said, "Hold on a minute, Hal" and turned and went back inside. When he came back, there was a lady with him. She had short dark hair with finger waves and wore a kitchen apron tied around her waist.

"I'd like you to meet my wife. Carol, this is Hal Brennan and his nephew Justin. They live out near the end of the road."

"Very nice to meet you, ma'am," Uncle Hal said.

Mr. Sadler said, "This is for you, Justin." And he held up a Nehi orange soda he had brought out with him. He reached into the pocket of his apron and took out a bottle opener. He popped off the cap and handed me the bottle. Nehi orange was my favorite.

"Thanks, Mister," I said. "It was nice meeting you both."

"All right," Uncle Hal said. "Get in the car then. See you next time, Mike." Hal started the car, and we drove away.

As we headed back to the ranch, Uncle Hal asked, "Where'd you run off to? You were supposed to wait by the car."

"I was just looking around. I was talking to another boy about my age. He said there's a school in Glory, a real school, but it's closed now because they don't have a teacher."

"That's about the gist of it. You might be able to go to that school next year if they do get a teacher. We'll think on it."

Hal didn't say any more about it. He didn't really say much more at all on the way back to the ranch. I mostly just sat there, too, drinking my orange Nehi and watching the scenery go by out the window. I thought it would be good to go to a real school. I had never really been to one before, and I wouldn't mind meeting some kids my age, like Wiley. He seemed like he might make a good friend. I liked Waters okay and even Uncle Hal most of the time, but they weren't friends. Hal was old, and even though Waters wasn't as old, he was still a grownup, and they were more like parents than friends I could talk to.

12

I thought some more about Hal and Waters, how both of them were grownups, and how it seemed I pretty much had to do what they told me. It was clear that Hal wasn't my daddy, but he always acted like he was in charge. It was his ranch and his house, after all. But he never put his arm around me, or patted me on the back or anything. He didn't seem to be able to do stuff like that. He could stroke Shorty's cheek and talk to him in a special way that made me see how much he loved that horse, but he couldn't be like that with folks, at least not with me. I wondered what he had been like with Orla. Maybe he was different back then.

Waters was easier to talk to, but he wasn't my daddy, either. He seemed more easy-going somehow, like he knew things were hard sometimes, but he had learned not to let things bother him. He could read his newspaper, sit on his porch and play his mouth harp and think about his apple trees. And that was enough. He always acted like things were okay, and that something good would come along eventually. I wished I could be like that. I admired his patience, too. Man had a lot of patience—willing to wait for years to see that tree grow all kinds of apples.

I didn't understand how Uncle Hal and Waters got along. They hardly talked to each other. Waters pretty much stayed in his cabin on top of the hill, stayed up there with his newspaper and his apple orchard, which occupied most of his time. Hal kept to the house, mostly, occasionally going into Glory for supplies. Sometimes he read the *Farm Journal* and talked about getting some cows and starting a little dairy herd. He really wasn't much for talking most of the time. The two of them kept to themselves, yet they seemed to communicate somehow. I thought there was something between them, but I couldn't figure out what it was.

One day Waters just said, out of the blue, "Hal says you might be able to go to school in the fall. How you plan on getting there?"

"I don't know. I hadn't really thought about it. They didn't have a teacher, last I heard. They get one yet?"

"I haven't heard. Hal just said it might be you could go to school in the fall."

"Well, how do the other kids get there then?"

"I s'pose the kids who live in town just walk to school. Probably the farm kids nearby ride their horses to school. Maybe ones that live farther out drive their kids to school."

"I don't think anybody's farther out than we are. We're the last ones at this end of the road."

"Road runs both ways from Glory, but you right about this end. And that's why I think you should start learning to drive," Waters said.

When I heard him say that, you could have knocked me over with a feather. "Really?" I said.

"If you're gonna go to school, that'd probably be best. But it's not something to take lightly. You old enough to drive, but you got to understand it's a big step. That car really belonged to your daddy. Hal and me drive that car, but it was your daddy's car. 'Bout the only thing you have left from your daddy. Be a shame if you didn't understand that and treat it with some respect."

"I guess I know that. I understand what you're saying, I think."

"Good. I always thought you were a sensible boy. You

always so quiet and all. Maybe it's just because you around old people all the time and haven't had a chance to act foolish like other kids do."

One morning, not long after that, Waters started teaching me to drive. We walked down the path from his cabin, and I slid the big barn door open all the way. Waters backed the Model A out of the barn, and pointed it toward the end of the road. Then he shut it off, got out of the car, and said, "Now it's your turn. Climb in," and he walked around to the other side of the car.

I stepped up on the running board and slid into the driver's seat, just like I had done before when it was parked in the barn. It was different now, though. I really wanted to drive, but when it came down to it, I was a little scared.

Waters looked at me and said, "All right, you probably worried a little bit about doing this. But you already know a lot about driving a car. You ridden in a car, this car, lots of times. You watched your Daddy drive it. You seen Hal drive it, and you seen me drive it. You watched us, you already know more than you think. Look around the car first. Look under the dash. What do you see?"

I looked under the dash. "There's a little spigot under there." I'd never really noticed, but I had seen Hal reach under the dash when he started the car in the morning.

"That's right. That turns on the gas. Gas is in a tank in the dash, but you got to turn on the faucet to make the gas flow. Go ahead."

I turned the handle on the spigot. "Now what?"

"Look over here," Waters said, pointing to a knob that stuck out on the right side below the dash. "This here's the choke rod. When the motor's cold, you turn it to the left a quarter turn. That changes the mixture of gas and air in the carburetor. Makes it easier to start — more gas, less air. Then you pull the whole rod out as far as it goes. It's got a spring on it. When the motor starts, let go of the choke. Go ahead now. You do it."

I took the knob and twisted it to the left, like Waters said, then pulled on the knob and the whole rod came out a little ways and then stopped. When I let go of the knob, the lever snapped back. "Like that?"

"Yeah, just like that. Now look at the steering wheel. You see the two levers sticking out on the sides? Left one's for the spark and the right one's for the throttle. Push the spark rod all the way up. Then pull the throttle down a couple of notches. We call it retarding the spark and advancing the throttle."

I did as Waters had said. "Now what?" I asked.

"Now turn the key on," he said pointing to the key that hung from the little cluster of instruments in the center of the dash. "Then look down to the floor. When you step on the little round pedal, it will make the starter motor turn the engine over. When it does, you'll hear the engine catch and start to run. When you hear that, then let go of the choke, and pull the spark lever down. The motor should run on its own."

I turned on the key, then pressed on the pedal. The starter made a grinding noise, and then the engine took off. I let go of the choke rod, and pulled down on the spark lever.

"Now turn the knob on the choke lever back to the right,"

When I turned the knob back, the engine ran smoother. By this time, I felt pretty worn out. "That's a lot to remember just to get started. We haven't even gone anywhere."

"Don't worry. That was the easy part. Besides,

you don't have to do all of that each time. Only when the motor's cold and you first start it up." Waters pointed out the emergency brake lever and the clutch and brake and gas pedals on the floor. "Now comes the hard part," he said.

Waters showed me how to let off the emergency brake by pulling back on the lever then pushing down on the button on the end and pushing the whole lever forward until it wouldn't go any further. Then he explained about the gearshift and the different positions it could take, said it was like the letter H, and for now all I needed to do was to put it in first gear, which meant moving the lever to the left and back. Finally, he told me to put my feet on the brake pedal and the clutch. He made me press down on the brake and then press in on the clutch and hold it down. Then, with Waters' help, I shifted into first gear and released the emergency brake.

"Now," he said, "let up on the clutch pedal a little bit at a time until the car starts to move. When you feel it move, let up on the brake and press the gas pedal."

The first time I tried, the engine stalled, and the car leaped forward and then stopped. I restarted the engine and tried again. This time the car stuttered and jerked forward, but it kept running after I gave it a little gas. Once we were rolling along, Waters told me to take hold of the shift lever, and then he put his hand on top of mine. He had me go faster, then put in the clutch, and he moved my hand on the shift lever so I could feel it go into the next gear. We started and stopped a bunch of times. Each time I got a little better, a little smoother at letting out the clutch.

When I thought I was doing pretty good, he made me stop halfway up a little hill. When I tried to take off again, the car started rolling backward when I tried to let out the clutch. I let it out too fast and stalled again. But after a while I figured it out and managed to take off going uphill without rolling back or stalling—at least not very often.

Waters made me turn the car around. He tried having me back up a ways, steering with one hand as I braced myself with the other and looked out the back window, but I had trouble with the steering, so we stopped. All of a sudden, I was really tired, and Waters seemed to know it. We changed places, then, and Waters drove back to the barn. I watched the way he drove and thought how easy he made it look. But so did Uncle Hal and so had Daddy. Driving seemed hard, but if everyone else could do it, I probably could, too. It wasn't hard for me to imagine myself sailing along with the windshield opened out a little and the breeze washing over me as I drove by myself, taking in the sights along the Glory Road.

For a while after that, Waters would find excuses to take the car out every so often and let me drive at least part of the way wherever we went. Waters never went into town, but we sometimes drove up to the end of the road and then hiked down to the river to fish. One time we drove down the road a ways to where an old railroad right-of-way crossed the Glory Road. We got out and hiked along the abandoned track to see where it went. "That's an old mine up ahead. Looks like it played out years ago—everything falling apart like it is," Waters said. We didn't get very close, but Waters pointed out the head frame sticking up and the hoist house, some of the buildings, and the piles of tailings. The buildings had rusty tin roofs that sagged here and there, and most of them looked like they were about to collapse. "Be best not to go pokin' around in that place. You liable to fall down that shaft or get squashed under one of those buildings if it give way with you inside." I wanted to go closer and look around, but Waters didn't think it was all that interesting, so we headed back to the car.

13

It was summer. The hills were still green from the spring rains, and the willows leafed out along the creek. The water in the creek ran clear every day, and the skies were mostly blue, with only a few white clouds here and there. The apple blossoms had slowly turned into apples on Waters' newly-pruned old trees, and he was happier than a clam at high tide. Most of the grafts on his "All-American" had taken off and were sprouting new green leaves. He managed to find some wooden boxes in the back of the barn that somebody else had used to pick apples, probably back when the old trees were in their prime. He hauled them out of the barn, inspected them, washed them, and repaired a few that were broken. He wanted to be ready when the apples started to ripen.

Uncle Hal fixed up the barn for the cows he was planning to raise. He built a gate in front of the milk barn to let the cows in and out of the pasture. When the gate was closed, the cows wouldn't be able to get out of the pasture. When the gate was opened, it swung over and latched to another fence that Hal added in front of the barn door, creating a kind of chute that led into the barn and would keep them from wandering into the road.

One day, Uncle Hal got up early, went out to the barn and came out after a while riding Shorty. He headed off down the Glory Road, just riding along like it was a pleasure ride until he disappeared from sight.

He was gone most of the day, but he came back in the evening, walking Shorty at that same leisurely pace. I had kind of been looking out for him all day. I finally spotted him when I was stacking firewood on the porch and saw him a ways off, coming up the road. When he got closer, I could see that he was leading a couple of cows on a rope behind him. The cows were taking their time, like cows always seem to do, moving along at a steady pace. I caught up with him as he passed by the house on his way to the barn.

"Where you been all day?" I asked, walking beside them. "Where'd the cows come from?"

"They're from the Weatherby place down the road a ways. I drove the Model A down there the other day when you and Waters were off doing something. They're milk cows. Thought it would be nice to have milk and butter once in a while again. Don't have a trailer to haul them in, so old man Weatherby got his neighbor to meet me half way, and now here we are."

I hadn't heard that much talk in one stretch from Uncle Hal in a long time. I figured it meant he was pretty pleased with himself about the whole thing. It would have been nice if he'd shared his plan with me. When he did things like this, I felt left out, like I wasn't important. He rode on, then, toward the barn. I followed along behind.

On the other side of the barn from where the Model A was, there was a smaller door that led into the barn. It wasn't really a door that closed or opened. It was just an opening in the barn wall that led into a part of the barn that had been built for milking cows. Uncle Hal tied Shorty to the fence beside the barn and led the cows inside. There was a row of stanchions for the cows with a long trough on the other side. Uncle Hal got the cows locked into the stanchions, and then he went back outside. He took the saddle off Shorty and parked it on the top fence rail. Then he untied Shorty and let him out into the pasture. He swung the gate over to the new fence he had added so the cows couldn't get out on the road.

When he came back inside with the saddle, he said, "C'mere, Justin. Let me show you what to do."

I didn't know much about cows, but I guessed I was about to add to the little I knew. I thought I had all the chores I needed to keep me busy. It looked like Hal didn't think so. We went through a little gate inside the barn and got down a bale of hay. Hal took down a hay knife that hung from one of the beams and split the bale of hay into smaller pieces that he spread in the trough. Then he opened an old flat top steamer trunk sitting at the end of the trough and propped the lid with a stick. "Keeps out the rats and mice. Make sure you always close the lid when you're done." The trunk was half filled with oats and barley. He picked up a coffee can inside the trunk and scooped out a full can and spread it out on top of the hay in the trough. All this attention seemed to please the cows, who just stood there chewing happily, their tails swinging back and forth to swat the occasional fly that crawled on their backs.

"These here are heifers, born last summer. We'll fatten 'em up a bit, and then when they get to be about fourteen months old, we'll take them back to Weatherby's for breeding. Then next summer we'll have calves we can eat in the fall and more milk and butter than we can shake a stick at."

Uncle Hal was an old man, but he must've thought he had plenty of time left, since he expected to wait a year and a half for milk and butter. He had as much patience as Waters, apparently. They were in some kind of standoff, those two, like they were each trying to out-wait the other. I wondered what it was all about, but I couldn't figure it out on my own. I supposed if I was as patient as they were, I would eventually find out.

14

Uncle Hal and I didn't have much to talk about, but Waters and I kept up on the news in the paper and on the radio. We despaired over the Hindenburg crash in May and then marveled over the Golden Gate Bridge opening later that month. It seemed like it was always boom or bust with the news. Dust storms raged through the Midwest one month. The next month we listened to the James J. Braddock—Joe Louis fight. Waters couldn't wait for the newspaper to come out on that story. I didn't know much about boxing, but I was kind of rooting for the Cinderella Man, Braddock, mostly to get at Waters, who was for the Brown Bomber all the way. He was so happy the way it turned out he could hardly wait till the paper came to paste the news clippings on his wall.

Ten days later, the news was all about Amelia Earhart—how she got lost trying to fly 'round the world. That's what I mean about boom and bust. The news is mostly bad, seems to me. I'd much rather listen to the *Lone Ranger*. "A fiery horse with the speed of light, a cloud of dust, and a hearty Hi-Yo Silver." I liked the way the announcer talked about "his faithful Indian companion, Tonto," and invited us to "Return with us now to those thrilling days of yesteryear." Then he would end with "The Lone Ranger rides again!" The world seemed like it was mostly bad news, but the Lone Ranger and Tonto always caught the bad guys, and everything was all right by the time the program ended.

I liked *The Shadow*, too. When the announcer asked, "Who knows what evil lurks in the hearts of men?" I was always ready to answer, "The Shadow knows," and laugh that creepy laugh along with him. And then, at the end of the show, he would remind us, "The weed of crime bears bitter fruit. Crime does not pay," and then there would be this long pause, and he'd finally say, "The Shadow knows!" How could you beat that?

Everybody knew there was a lot of really bad stuff going on in the world, and plenty of bad things had happened to us, too, when we were back at the mill. We knew Father Coughlin and Hitler were giving the Jewish people a hard time, for instance. But it was nice sometimes to think about other things, and those programs made life more interesting on the Glory Road, where nothing very interesting ever seemed to happen.

The mail came only once a week, and Waters was always on the lookout for Sully when he brought the newspaper. Sully usually showed up in the early afternoon, and he and Waters would talk for a while before Sully turned around and headed back toward town. If I was around, I usually left them alone to talk. Waters would want to go in and read his newspaper after Sully left anyway, so there wasn't much point in my hanging around.

One week when he and Waters were talking, Sully had stayed quite a bit longer than usual, and I wondered what that had been all about. Theirs was mostly a meet-and-greet kind of talk, with a little news and weather thrown in, that didn't last more than ten minutes or so. But this time Sully stayed about half an hour, and I wondered what was up.

The next day, after I had done my chores, which now included feeding Hal's new heifers, I walked up the hill to Waters' cabin. He was out in the orchard checking on his apples. Some of the early apples were starting to get ripe, and he checked on them nearly every day.

"How they coming?" I asked.

"These here 'bout ready," he said. He had his pocketknife out, and he was getting ready to cut one of the apples open. He took the knife and made a long cut all the way around the apple. Then he folded the knife closed against his thigh and put the knife back in his pocket. He put the apple between his palms and then twisted them in opposite directions, neatly separating the apple into two nearly equal halves. He poked at the seeds inside the apple halves. "Yes sir, we could start picking these any time now. Put some in the apple house and maybe make cider out of the others."

"How are you gonna make cider?" I asked.

"Sully was telling me that those Weatherby folk got a press down to their place. Said he saw it out beside their barn. I was wonderin' if we could maybe borrow it or something. We got some crocks and a couple of barrels out in the barn. I found 'em when I moved all those boxes. You think maybe Hal would ask them? White folks probably find it pretty easy to say no to me, but Hal talked them out of those heifers. Thought maybe he could talk to them, maybe trade them some cider for the use of their press. "

"You could ask him. See what he says."

"Sully said he'd spread the word if we start making cider. Folks might drive out to buy a little."

"Could be. It would be nice to have some ourselves."

Somehow Waters talked Uncle Hal into asking Mr. Weatherby about the cider press. I wondered what he'd said to convince him. It didn't seem like something Uncle Hal would just agree to on his own. But the next day Hal asked me if I wanted to drive down the road to the Weatherby place with him. I asked him if I could drive the car. It would be my first time driving with him, but he said I could, so I was happy to go along.

The Weatherby house was a big, square two-story farmhouse with a wraparound sitting porch shaded by an overhanging roof propped up by skinny posts with scrollwork at the top corners. It looked really old, its white paint gone chalky with time.

No one had stayed long enough in Cooper's Gulch to grow old, and up to now Hal was my model for that description, but old man Weatherby was even older than Hal and, like the house, seemed to have gotten chalky, too, wispy white hair peeking out from under an old stained hat. He had on bib overalls washed nearly white, and walked with a cane.

Mrs. Weatherby wore a faded housedress and sat in an old wicker chair on the porch the whole time we were there.

A long gravel drive beside the house led to a white-painted barn in back. Various pieces of farm equipment were rusting away beside the barn. There was an old wagon with grass springing up through the spokes of its wooden wheels and a plow and a harrow beside it.

Through the open door I could see the front of an old tractor parked inside the shadowy interior. Most everything I saw, even the Weatherbys, seemed left over from another time.

Uncle Hal stepped out of the car, and Mr. Weatherby hobbled over to the car and leaned on the front fender as they talked. After a while, the two men walked to the barn at the end of the driveway, and I got out of the car and followed after them. They had gone around the side of the barn by the time I caught up to them. The contraption they were looking at had a wooden frame that stood on four legs. It had a hopper on one end, with a crank handle sticking out below it and two buckets made of slats joined together with metal straps that went all the way around each one. On the other end was a big screw with a wheel on top to turn it with. It was pretty easy to figure out how it worked. You just put the apples in the hopper and turned the crank handle, and the machinery inside would grind up the apples, which would fall in that bucket. Then you'd slide the bucket down to the other end and turn that wheel to squash the apples. The juice would drain down to the end where there was a little hole in the tray under the buckets, and you could catch the juice in a pan or crock or something. The whole thing was made of wood except for the handle and the gears and the big iron screw. On the side of the frame it said "Eagle, Jr." in black letters outlined in gold.

Hal said, "I thought you wouldn't mind, Ted. In fact, I thought you might think it was a pretty good idea. We'll take the press back to the ranch today, if that's okay with you." He looked at me, then back at Mr. Weatherby. "Then I'll drop by with that special cider when it's ready."

"Sounds good. Be lookin' forward to it. Go ahead and back your car up to the barn."

Uncle Hal turned the car around and backed it up along the side of the barn. We lifted and carried the heavy press over to the car. Hal took the spare tire off the back of the car, and we lifted the press over the top of the tire carrier so the frame of the press kind of hung on it, and then put a board on top of the bumper and rested two legs of the press on the board. We lashed the whole thing to the car and put the tire and the press buckets in the back seat. Hal drove home slowly, stopping twice to make sure the press wasn't going to fall off the car.

Waters was about as pleased with the cider press as Hal was with his heifers. He couldn't wait to try it out. I helped him as he cleaned it up, wiping away the dust and dirt that had settled on the press while it sat in Mr. Weatherby's barn. Waters sent me up the hill to fill a pail from the spring to wash the whole thing down. When I got back, he was putting a little grease on the big iron screw. He turned the wheel and moved the screw up and down a few times, and then he wiped off the extra grease with a rag. We washed the press and rinsed out the buckets that came with it. Waters dragged the crocks and barrels he found in the barn out to the apple house and stacked them along the wall. I made another trip to the spring so he could wash one of the crocks to hold the first batch of cider.

I helped him fill a few boxes of apples, gathering up some windfalls that looked pretty good and tossing them in, too. We carted the apples over to the press and rinsed them off. Together we scooped double handfuls out of the boxes and loaded the hopper till it wouldn't hold any more.

Waters slid one of the buckets underneath the hopper, and I turned the crank to start chopping up the apples. It was hard to turn at first as the teeth inside the machine bit into the apples, but got smoother as I kept cranking. Chunks of apple began raining into the bucket and the apples waiting their turn in the hopper bounced up and down as they sank lower and lower.

"Hold on, Justin," Waters said. I'd been so busy cranking the handle and watching the apples bob up and down in the hopper that I didn't notice that the bucket had filled and started to overflow. Waters slid the bucket down to the other end of the press, put a special wooden block that fit into the bucket on top of the chopped up apples, and started turning down the screw to squash them. He had put a big enamel pan under the hole at that end to catch the juice, and I watched as it streamed out of the spaces between the slats on the bucket.

While Waters emptied the juice from the pan into the crock, I cranked another batch of apples through the hopper. When we had filled the pan up a couple of times and Waters had transferred the juice to the crock, he went back to his cabin and returned with two cups so we could have a taste. He swatted at a couple of yellow jackets that were buzzing around as he dipped our cups in the apple juice. Then we toasted each other by clicking our cups together and taking a drink.

Waters looked up at me, smiling. "Fresh squeezed always taste the best. Nothing quite like it."

I couldn't argue with that.

Thursday morning, a couple days later, Hal told me it was time to sign up for school and took me into Glory. School was supposed to start on Monday. When we got there, the new teacher, a man named Mr. Phillips, wasn't there, but the lady who signed us up said he would be there when school started at eight-thirty on Monday morning.

When we left the school, Hal asked, "Are you hungry? I thought we might stop at the Bon Ton and have some lunch before we headed back to the ranch."

"Sure," I said. We'd never done anything like that before. Hal seemed to be in a generous mood. Getting signed up for school was a big deal for me. Maybe it was his idea of a celebration. But I was always hungry, and it was a long way back to the ranch.

The Bon Ton Café was located in an old two-story building across from the Rexall. Curtains in the upstairs windows probably meant there were apartments up there. A big picture window next to the entrance had the restaurant name painted in green letters on a white banner with scrolled ends.

Uncle Hal held the door open and I went inside. A cash register stood at one end of a long counter with a folding screen behind it that separated the area from the rest of the Bon Ton, which was really just one big room. A waitress behind the counter closed the drawer of the cash register, adding a receipt to others on a spiked holder beside it. She picked up menus from the other end of the counter and led us to a table.

On the left side, behind that folding screen, was a soda fountain with a gray marble countertop. A row of stools with padded tops lined the counter in front and a big mirror ran from one end to the other in back. In the middle of the counter was the soda bar, with fancy silver fittings and black handles sticking up from the counter. Along the back bar in front of the mirror, glasses for sodas and sundaes were stacked in pyramid-shaped piles. A bunch of bananas hung from a big hook on one end, and tall glass cylinders held long silver spoons and soda straws. Sugar cones with little paper sleeves separating them were stacked in a tray, and bottled sodas were lined up on the other end of the bar.

An older man and his wife sat at one of the tables lined up on the other side of the room. Overhead, black fans that hung down from long poles slowly stirred the air. The tables had black-and-white checkered tablecloths, and the wooden chairs were painted white with black padded seats. Some of the chairs were turned upside down on the tables, and a long-handled mop leaned against one of the tables. On the back wall, someone had hung two mounted deer heads. They were a little tattered and had cobwebs between the horns. They looked down on us with eyes dimmed a little by grease from the kitchen and the dust that clung to it.

Uncle Hal nodded a greeting to the folks at the other table, took off his hat, and hung it on the back of one of the other chairs.

"Used to be a nicer place, the Bon Ton," Uncle Hal said. "Orla liked to stop in here when we came into town. Turned a trip to town into an occasion. Orla was like that, always made ordinary things seem special."

He looked away when he said that. I knew he was thinking about other times. I spent a lot of time doing that myself. Uncle Hal had never talked about Orla before. Coming back to the ranch must have stirred up a lot of memories.

"Glory had more to look forward to when people had money in their pockets. Orla and I—we had plans, too. Then everything sort of came apart. Hard times all around now."

The waitress returned, setting two glasses of ice water on the table. She had on a blue checked dress with a round white collar and white trim on the short sleeves.

"My name's Billie," she said "How you folks doin' today?"

"We're just fine, thanks, Billie. My name's Hal, and this is my nephew Justin."

"Nice to meet both of you." She pulled a pad from the pocket of her apron and plucked a pencil from behind her ear. "What can I get for you today?"

Uncle Hal ordered a ham sandwich and coffee. I asked for a grilled cheese sandwich and an orange Nehi.

"Sounds good," Billie said. "Be just a minute." She went over to the wall with the deer heads, tore the slip from her pad, and put it under one of the little clips on the wheel that hung above the window that looked into the kitchen.

While we were waiting for our food, a man came out of the kitchen carrying two gallon jugs filled with some dark liquid and went behind the soda fountain. He bent down below the counter and was out of sight for a minute. Then he popped back up with two empty jugs. He set them on top of the counter, took out a rag, and began wiping some glasses, which he stacked on the back wall in front of the mirror. When he was done, he picked up the empty jugs and went back into the kitchen. He was gone for a bit and then returned, picked up the mop, and started pushing it around under the table with the upturned chairs.

I suddenly had an idea. "What do you think those jugs are for?" I asked Uncle Hal.

"Fountain syrup, most likely. For Cokes, and other drinks. They mix it with soda water to make the drinks."

"What do you think they do with those jugs when they're empty?"

"Don't know. Throw 'em out, probably."

"Waters could use those jugs for his cider, don't you think?"

"Not a bad idea. Let's ask that fella." Uncle Hal got the man's attention and called him over to the table. They talked about it some, and the man agreed that they had no use for the empty jugs.

"Take 'em if you can use 'em. We just throw 'em out. There's a bunch sittin' out back in their boxes. Come back later if you want more."

"Thank you," Hal said. "I think we might just do that."

Billie brought our food on thick china plates. The sandwiches were dressed up with a scoop of potato salad on a piece of lettuce and a long green slice of pickle on the side. Uncle Hal thanked her as she refilled his coffee cup, and we settled in to eating.

When we were finished, Uncle Hal drove the car around the back, and we loaded up four boxes of empty bottles that were stacked against the wall behind the Bon Ton. There were four jugs in each box, so Waters would have sixteen bottles to start with. I could probably get more of them when I came back to go to school.

Uncle Hal let me drive on the way back to the ranch. It was only my second time driving with him, but I was a lot better now than when I first started, and he didn't have anything bad to say about my driving. I didn't know what to think about school. I didn't know whether I was going to like the school, the teacher, or the other kids. But I thought the driving might be the best part of going to school every day.

When we got back to the ranch, I parked the Model A in the barn and trotted up the hill to tell Waters about the jugs. He was delighted with the news, and practically ran down the hill to help me unload them from the car. After we had got all the boxes up the path to his cabin, he quickly set about rinsing them out. Then he scalded the jugs and their caps with boiling water and set them out on the drainboard and the table to dry.

Waters filled a pan with cider and set it on his stove. He poked the coals in the firebox and added some wood, heating the pan almost to boiling, then setting it aside to cool.

"Call that pasteurizing—supposed to kill the germs."

Waters put a funnel in one of the jugs and covered it with clean cheesecloth. Then he dipped a metal cup into the warm cider and poured it through the cheesecloth to filter out some of the sediment and anything that might have gotten into the cider.

"Dirt and bugs don't usually do much to improve the flavor," he said, chuckling.

When the jug was full, Waters screwed the cap on loosely and set it on his drainboard to cool. "I'll tighten the cap after it cools down. Then wipe down the bottles before they go in the apple house."

He was starting to fill another jug when I remembered I had chores to do before supper and left him to his work

15

I got up early Monday morning. Uncle Hal had let me use his old Big Ben alarm clock, and I set it the night before. It ticked so loudly I had a hard time going to sleep. Finally, I set it on a pillow, which made the ticking less noticeable. I put the headphones from the crystal set over my ears and fell asleep listening to music.

I got up at six, dressed, and went out to the barn to feed Uncle Hal's heifers and make sure they were all right. I spread out the hay and scooped out the oats and barley. The watering trough beside the barn was fed from the spring on the hill above Waters' cabin, but I always looked to see that it was full and cleaned out the leaves and stuff that sometimes settled on top of the water. There was a salt lick beside the trough for the cows to work on when they were in the mood. Back at the house, I found Uncle Hal at the kitchen table, hunched over his coffee cup. He wasn't much for talking, especially before he'd had his coffee. I made a lunch to take to school while he sat there with his morning thoughts. I fried an egg and put a slice of bread in the pan afterward to toast it a bit. I watched it carefully to keep it from burning. When it looked as if it was starting to smoke a little, I flipped it over, and did the other side. After it was all on the plate, I sat at the table opposite Uncle Hal and spooned out some jam from the little pot on the table by the sugar bowl.

"First day at school got you worried?" Hal asked.

"A little bit, I guess. It's just that everything's new. I've never been to a real school, but I'm glad you got me signed up." I took a bite of the toast, wiping a little jelly off the corner of my mouth with my napkin. "It was nice stopping for lunch at the Bon Ton, too. I never went to a real restaurant, either."

"A little different from the cookhouse in Cooper's Gulch, wasn't it?"

"Sure was—but it was nice. I wouldn't mind going there again."

"Maybe we'll do that sometime, try one of their ice cream sodas."

Uncle Hal put down his cup down and looked at me. "Don't fret about school. Just listen more than you talk. Keep your eyes open and watch what the other kids do. Probably take you a while, but you'll fit in fine. Keep your eyes on the road when you're driving, too."

About seven-thirty, I put my dishes in the sink and gathered up my things. I put on a jacket and headed for the door. When I said goodbye to Uncle Hal, he wished me luck and reminded me again to be careful driving. I wondered if he was worried about me. He never said much to me in the morning, but he seemed to be positively chatty today.

When I got to the barn, I slid open the big door and got into the car. I started it up, going through the routine Waters had taught me. I let it run a little while, then backed slowly out the door and down the ramp to the road. I was afraid of going too fast and losing control, but the ramp was covered with frost, and when I hit the brake to slow down, the wheels locked, and the car slid down the ramp instead. I didn't know what to do, but my foot was still on the brake pedal when the tires hit the road, and the car stopped skidding. My heart rattled around in my chest for a bit before it settled down. Then I backed around carefully, pointing it toward town. I hauled back on the emergency brake and went back to close the barn door.

Nothing else scared me on the drive into town. The morning sun was behind me, the weather was fine, and it was kind of fun driving by myself in the car. The trees along the road rushed by, and everything I passed seem new. I knew it wouldn't always be fun, though. I figured it was one thing to be able to drive. It would be different when I had to drive. And driving this road twice a day in the winter might get pretty darn old. But today it felt good, really good.

When I got to town, I slowed down and looked around as I drove down Main Street. At the feed store a man was sweeping up some spilled grain on the loading dock, and another man with a necktie and red suspenders, probably Mr. McManus himself, stood in the open doorway that led to the warehouse in back. He had a tote board in hand and was staring at a stack of boxes piled at one side of the dock. Across the street, the Bon Ton was doing a land office business. All the parking spaces in front were filled, most of them with pickup trucks, and two men were coming out, toothpicks in the corners of their mouths. Breakfast must be their busy time. Sadler's Market didn't look to be open yet, but Mike was outside in his green apron, sweeping the sidewalk again. I'd only seen him twice now, and he was sweeping the sidewalk both times. Something he did every morning, I guessed. Must like to keep his store neat. I could admire that. As I came up to the corner, Al was wiping his hand on that red rag he carried in his pocket, about to "he'p" a lady in a blue roadster parked by the pumps.

When I got to the corner, I stopped to check for cars on the side road, but I needn't have bothered. No cars were coming either way. There were some kids coming down the street, probably headed for school. I made a right turn at the stop sign and drove down to the school.

Some horses were tied to a railing on the far side of

the building and a few more cars were parked on the street than when I was there before. I found a place down the street a ways from the school. I'd seen a spot across from the school between two cars, but I didn't know how to park that way, and I didn't want to embarrass myself in front of the other kids and a few parents who were standing around, holding little ones by the hand.

Older kids sat on the low walls on each side of the wide steps that led up to the double doors. I crossed the street and walked back to the schoolhouse. When I spotted Wiley sitting at the bottom of the steps, I waved at him, and he got up and started walking down the street to meet me. When I got closer, I asked him how he'd been doing. He'd been wearing overalls and sneakers the first time I saw him, but today he had on long pants and a sweater vest, with a white shirt underneath. He looked uncomfortable.

"Okay, I guess," he said. "I'd be better if this weren't the first day of school. School's 'bout my least favorite thing."

"I know what you mean," I said. Only that was a lie. I'd never been close enough to a real school that I could go to it on a regular basis. I didn't think Miss Garvey's "lessons" were going to count for much, but I could see Wiley was a little pained about losing his freedom, so I was trying to tread lightly. I needed a friend, and he seemed a likely prospect.

The other kids were a pretty mixed group, sort of like a come-as-you-are party. Everyone just wore what they had, I guess. Most of the girls wore dresses of some sort, though the little ones were probably wearing grownup clothes that had been cut down and remade. Some of the littler boys wore knickers, though hardly anybody wore those anymore. I thought maybe they'd been made from cut down men's pants. The older boys mostly wore overalls, but some, like Wiley, had been made to dress up a little by their mothers. The older girls wore dresses, gingham or plaid, with skirts that ended above the ankles. They wore ankle socks with saddle shoes, but some had on moccasins with no socks at all.

About then the door to the school opened, and a skinny, middle-aged man with wire-rimmed glasses stepped out onto the porch. He looked sternly at the kids who were waiting to go inside, looked up and down the street as well. He had a hand bell in his right hand, and he gave it a shake. Then he turned around and walked back inside. All the kids looked at each other for a minute. Then, one by one, they followed him. Wiley and me went in, too.

There was a kind of vestibule inside with a door on the right that opened into a walk-in coat closet. Beyond that double doors opened into the classroom, a really big room that was even bigger than the dining hall at the mill. It had a high ceiling that showed the beams and rafters under the roof and four big windows on each long sidewall let in lots of light. There was a raised stage on one end, closed off with a tall curtain. Right then I remembered that this was sometimes a church, and I thought that explained a lot about how it looked.

Three rows of tables had been set up across the room near the front, nine tables in all. Two chairs at each table faced the stage, and there was enough space to walk between the tables. The others took seats as they came in. Wiley and me were last. We sat in the second row at the same table. When everybody was seated, the teacher waited until everybody quieted down. Then he cleared his throat and spoke.

"Good morning, everyone. I am Mr. Phillips, your new teacher. Every morning when I ring the bell, you will file into this classroom and take your seats in an orderly manner. You will remove your hats and coats and leave them in the closet by the door. There will be no eating or drinking, no chewing or spitting in this room. Do you understand?"

There was a lot of head bobbing and a few "Yes, sirs" in answer to his question. He repeated it one more time. "Do I make myself clear or not?"

This time most everybody said, "Yes, sir," and he seemed to be satisfied. He went on to ask, "How many of you have attended this school before? Raise your hands, please."

Most of the others raised their hands, but there were a couple others besides me that didn't. There were two older boys at the table next to me and Wiley that looked to be about twenty years old. They reminded me of some of the younger men I had known at Cooper's Gulch, but they were a lot cleaner and looked like they had shaved more recently. There were some little ones at one of the front tables that looked to be about seven or eight. The rest were various ages in between.

Mr. Phillips picked up a sheet of paper and told us to print our names on the paper if we knew how and then to pass the paper to the person beside us. It took a while for the paper to make its way around the room. I watched as it went from hand to hand and table to table and counted fourteen including the two older ones. After we had written our names and passed the paper back to him, he asked us all to stand and say the Pledge of Allegiance. There was a flag in a brass stand on the left side of the stage. On the wall beside the flag was a printed copy of the pledge, which was good for me since Miss Gravy had apparently neglected that part of our schooling.

Mr. Phillips asked if one of us would like to lead the others in saying it. One of the girls in the front, a red-haired girl with freckles who looked to be about fourteen or fifteen, raised her hand and stood up. She had on a green plaid dress with a matching ribbon in her hair. She looked around to see if we were paying attention and put her hand over her heart. Then she turned to face the flag standing on the stage. We all placed our hands over our hearts and turned toward the flag, too. The girl started us off with, "I pledge allegiance," and we followed along, muddling through the rest of it till we got to "and justice for all." Then Mr. Phillips said, "Please be seated," and we sat down again.

"We will begin each day with the Pledge of Allegiance," he said. Then he read off each of our names, and when somebody said, "Here", he paused and looked directly at the person like he was trying to memorize their face. He asked each of us if we had gone to this school last year. If a student said yes, he asked them how old they were and what grade they were in last year, and he wrote down their answers next to their names.

The two older boys said they were nineteen and twenty, but that they hadn't been to school very much. Curt Spencer said he had to work 'cause their Pa ran off, and they didn't have much money. The other one, Jesse Wheelock, said they moved around a lot when he was little, and then, when they got settled in one place, his folks needed him to help out on the farm.

Mr. Phillips told them, "The school has no obligation to teach students your age. However, if you behave yourselves, you may attend as you are able. I will do what I can to provide you with useful instruction."

When he got to me, I told Mr. Phillips about the mill and how there were only four of us children, and how Miss Garvey had tried to help us out. I explained about how we came here last year when there was no teacher, and said how I was willing to give it a try if he was.

Mr. Phillips thanked us for sharing our life stories, and then he divided us up, mostly according to how old we were. He sent each group back to the coat room to hang up their things and then told us where he wanted us to sit. He put the youngest ones in front where he could keep an eye on them; the ones who were a little older ended up in the middle row, with Wiley and me at the end. Curt and Jesse ended up behind us. The rest of the seats in the last row were empty.

When everybody was finally settled, Mr. Phillips passed out some books that had stories in them. He showed us the page to turn to, and then he asked us, one at a time, to read out of the book, if we could. Some of the little ones squirmed in their seats when they were called on. They hemmed and hawed for a while, and said they couldn't do it 'cause the words were too hard, but most of the ones who were a little older could read fairly well. Wiley showed he had the hang of it when it was his turn, but I didn't do as well. Reading the newspaper articles with Waters had helped some, but I still stumbled a lot when I read. The two older boys could hardly read at all, but Mr. Phillips wasn't too hard on them. All in all, I thought he was all right. He was just trying to figure out who he'd been saddled with. He was starting at a disadvantage, too, and he didn't make anyone feel bad for not knowing.

We all took our pails and sacks outside when it was lunchtime. Most of the other kids knew each other, and they went off in groups of two or three to sit with their friends and eat.

The littler boys and girls mostly kept to themselves. There was a lot of horseplay and teasing, running around and squealing. No wonder they had trouble sitting still in class.

Agnes Wheelock and Annie Sadler, the daughter of the man who owned the grocery store, shared a long bench under a big oak with a couple younger girls. Agnes and Annie were the same age as Wiley and me, as I discovered with the help of Mr. Phillips.

Annie was small and dark and pretty, in a boyish kind of way. She had a little spritz of freckles on her nose and cheeks and dark brown eyes that reminded me of Flag, our deer. I thought she was nice. She didn't say much in class except when Mr. Phillips called on her, but her voice was soft when she spoke. She seemed smart enough to be comfortable in class, unlike Wiley and me.

Wiley said he usually went home for lunch, but brought his lunch today, thinking I might like to have somebody to eat with on the first day. I thought that was pretty nice of him, considering that he had no way of knowing whether I'd show up or not. He asked me if I wanted to come to his house for lunch sometime. "It's just down the street."

I remembered the green house with the picket fence. "I'd like that," I said.

"I have to ask Ma first, but I'm sure it will be okay. I'll let you know what she says".

In the afternoon, Mr. Phillips tried to find out what we knew in the way of adding and subtracting, if we knew our times tables and such. Most of us could count, though some of the little ones kept using their fingers to do it. He put a few different problems on the board and asked us to try and work as many of them as we could.

After a while he collected the papers. He looked at them a while, made a frowny kind of face, and then put them on his desk.

Mr. Phillips looked up from the papers, pushed his glasses up on his nose, and said, "As you probably know, most of you are at different places in reading and in math. I expected as much, because of the differences in your ages, and, of course, because not all of you have been able to attend school regularly. I will do what I can to help each of you.

Starting tomorrow I will begin to work with you in groups. I will work hard to help you. If you make a genuine effort and come to school every day, you will be rewarded for your hard work. Learning is hard work, but knowing is a lot of fun."

Mr. Phillips had seemed kind of gruff at first, but he also seemed like he really wanted us to learn. By the end of the day, he probably figured out he had picked a tough row to hoe when he signed on to teach in Glory. I didn't know about the other kids, but I thought I would give him a chance. The first day of school was probably as hard on him as it was on us.

When he let us go in the afternoon, the little kids ran out the door and down the steps, laughing and poking at each other. Most of the others just went walking off in different directions. Wiley and me sat at the bottom of the steps and talked a while. We watched the red-haired girl walk over to where the horses were. She put her things in a saddle bag before mounting her horse, a nice-looking black mare with a white blaze on its forehead.

"That's Agnes Wheelock," Wiley said. "She thinks she's smarter than everybody else. She might be, for all I know. Her brother's not so smart, though. He's one of those two older boys that sat in the back with us. Probably just came to school 'cause it was the first day, and his old man wanted him to look after his sister. They live way out in the hills at a place called Fowler's Rock. Everybody pretty much stays away from Jesse Wheelock. I think he's just smart enough to know how dumb he is, and when he found out, it made him mad. He's the meanest kid in the whole school."

Just then Jesse Wheelock and the other older kid came out and walked past us down the steps together. As they headed out to where the horses were tied, Wiley said, "That's Curt Spencer," "Doesn't know beans when the bag is open, either. He ain't so bad by himself, but when he's with Jesse, it's hard to tell them apart."

After they passed us, Jesse turned back and looked at me like I was fresh meat and he was hungry.

"You'd be best off if you just stayed away from them two. Take it from me."

I thanked Wiley for the advice. We watched as Jesse and Curt walked over to the horses, untied them, and mounted up. They rode off, following Agnes, who had ridden off without waiting for them.

After I left Wiley, I walked back to the car and just sat inside for a few minutes. It was warm sitting in the afternoon sun. I rolled down the window on my side and undid the knobs on each side of the windshield, pushing the bottom out a few inches to let in some air. I sat there, resting my hands on the steering wheel, and thought about my first day at school.

It had been a long one for everyone, it seemed to me. The little kids had fussed and fidgeted, hard-pressed to sit still that long. Wiley had complained to me about losing his freedom, but surrendered to the familiar routine without putting up much of a fight. Old hands like Agnes Wheelock and Annie Sadler were happy to have a new teacher.

I was nervous, at first, being new. But Mr. Phillips was new, too, and he seemed to take a real interest in the kids, even Curt and Jesse, who didn't seem too happy to be there. I thought Mr. Phillips was okay, but I was still relieved to have had Wiley there to help me sort it all out.

When I got home, Waters was doing something down the road by his mailbox. I put the Model A in the barn and went to see what he was doing. When I caught up to him, I saw that he was sinking a fence post in the ground beside the path that led from his mailbox up to his cabin.

He looked up when he heard me coming. "Hey, Justin. How was school? You feel any smarter than you were this morning?"

I knew when he was teasing. "I don't think so—probably take me a week or so to notice. It was okay, though. The teacher, Mr. Phillips, seemed all right. There's fifteen of us altogether. A few my age, some younger, a couple older ones, too. What are you doing?"

"Just gettin' ready for business. I'm gonna put up this post and nail a board on top of it. Then I'm gonna put one of those jugs on top so when folks come up the road, looking to buy some cider or some apples, they know where to stop."

"You could sleep in the middle of the road without worrying about getting run over. What makes you think people are suddenly going to come out this way looking to buy apple cider?"

"Sully say he spread the word all the way to Glory and all around where he deliver the newspapers and the mail. I gotta be ready when the time come."

I supposed advertising might help, but I couldn't see a crowd of people driving all that way to buy apples or cider. I wished him luck.

"Take more than just luck. You wait and see. People be coming out here with picnic baskets, bringing their kids with them and all."

I thought he was dreaming. But it seemed to make him happy, so I didn't say anything more about it. If it was really true, Waters must know something I didn't know.

16

By the middle of September, driving to school and back became part of my daily routine. I got up early, took the car out in the dark, turned on the headlights, and drove to school. Sometimes in the morning the fog hung along the creek and made it hard to see. I'd come to a narrow spot where the road turned as it followed a bend in the creek, and the whole road just disappeared in a cloud of white. Even though the Model A had big nickel-plated headlamps with silver-plated reflectors behind the glass lenses, they didn't really throw much light on the road ahead. But by now I could have driven the Glory Road in the dark or in the fog with my eyes closed. I knew when to slow down for the little potholes and when to drive around the big ones. Once or twice a week, on the way home, I remembered to check behind the Bon Ton for the syrup jugs and brought them home to Waters.

Although we made fun of him sometimes, Mr. Phillips turned out to be a pretty good teacher. He was patient and kind most of the time, and I was learning more than I ever could have learned from old Miss Gravy, even though she tried. Some of the kids weren't so nice. The ten and twelve year-olds, especially Todd Andrews and Amos Weatherby, old Mr. Weatherby's grandson, delighted in pestering Tommy or Alice or Aaron, hiding the little kids' things or stealing from their lunch pails when the younger ones weren't looking. Mr. Phillips' favorite punishment was to cut about three feet off a roll of wallpaper he kept behind his desk and make the offenders write "I will not steal from

Tommy's lunch pail," or whatever they had done, over and over until they had filled up the blank side of the paper from top to bottom. Amos must have been slow to learn 'cause he got the treatment several times, but his penmanship was improving.

Wiley and me avoided trouble with Jesse and Curt mostly by staying away from them, but Wiley had taken a liking to Agnes, even though he thought she was stuck-up, and I could see trouble coming sooner or later.

After Wiley's ma had said it was okay, I went to Wiley's house for lunch one day. They had a really nice house. I think it was the cleanest place I ever saw. Mrs. Travers had doilies all over everywhere. Made me nervous to sit on her sofa with those big antimacassars on the back. But Wiley's mother was real nice and didn't make me feel bad about my manners or anything. I was just always nervous I might break something.

After we ate, Wiley wanted to show me the backyard, so we went out to take a look around. Mrs. Travers told him not to spend too much time out there because we had to go back to school in a little while. Wiley said we wouldn't be long, and we went out through the laundry room and down the steps behind the house. The yard was really deep. A driveway along the right side of the house led to a little barn in the back. Wiley said that was where his pa kept his horseshoeing supplies and such. A rail fence that came out from the left side of the barn went around behind it to form a little area big enough for a horse or two.

Closer to the house there was a woodshed with firewood piled high inside and a chopping block with an axe stuck in it just inside the open doorway. Off to the side against the wall stood an old grindstone mounted in a wood frame that had a seat on one end where you could sit and sharpen an axe or a hatchet.

A clothesline was strung between posts beside the woodshed. It must not have been washday because the clothesline was empty. A picnic table sat under a little tree that gave it some shade. Wiley said that sometimes when it was hot in the house, they ate outside at the table.

Further out in the yard, opposite the barn, was a garden patch, pretty empty now, except for some squash and a few pumpkins and a couple rows of cabbage on one end and a pile of cornstalks that had been cut down and laid to one side.

A chicken house stood next to the garden; it had a little yard in front that was fenced in and covered with chicken wire. Wiley wanted to show me the chickens before we had to go back. About a dozen or so, of various sizes and colors, clucked and pecked and strutted around the little yard.

"Chickens are interesting," he said. "They're all different, got different personalities. That banty hen over there? She's little, but she don't put up with any guff from the bigger chickens. Acts like she's just as big as the rest of them. Maybe she don't know she ain't. They try anything with her, she chases them around the yard.

"That big rooster is mean as heck, chased me around the yard when I was littler. Look at the spurs on 'im. He scares me still. Anyway, we keep the chickens mostly for the eggs. They roost in their house at night so the 'coons and foxes and skunks won't bother 'em. Let 'em out in the morning and collect the eggs while they're still warm. I try not to get too attached to them since we eat one of the chickens now and then. Maybe when we got some chicks, you could take some, raise chickens out to your place."

"I'd have to ask Uncle Hal, but that sounds pretty

good to me."

About then, Wiley's mother called us in, and we hurried back to the house.

By the third week of school, I relaxed enough to accept Mrs. Travers' invitation to come home with Wiley for lunch on Wednesdays. She said it made a nice change in the middle of the week. I was working on her to let Wiley ride home with me and stay at the ranch over the weekend, but she hadn't wanted to say yes without meeting my folks. I explained that I didn't exactly live with my parents, only my mother's uncle Hal and a man named Waters who had been my daddy's friend before he died. It was awkward. I could see why she was hesitating, but I thought I might eventually win her over.

Sometimes Hal asked me to pick up something at Sadler's on the way home from school. The store wasn't really big, but it seemed that way to me. Cooper's Gulch never really had a store, so this was new territory for me.

I liked the smell of the oiled wood floor that greeted me when I walked in the door. A meat display case with a sloping front stood to the left beside the counter where Mr. Sadler kept his adding machine and rang up his sales. On the right side a longer counter with glass-fronted bins stretched toward the back of the store. Behind the glass were several kinds of beans, coffee, dried peas, macaroni, and such. An old-fashioned coffee grinder with big red flywheels that went round when you turned the handle sat on the countertop. Some of the bins held penny candies—jelly beans, lemon drops, horehound, salt water taffy, and licorice drops.

Refrigerated cases with soda pop and beer, milk and cheese and butter stood against the back wall. Three rows of shelves held flour and sugar and canned goods with fancy labels. There were jams and jellies and little baskets of potatoes and yams and onions. It was a lot to take in all at once.

When I went inside, setting the bell over the door tinkling, I often found Annie working in the store, wearing a green apron like her father's. I had, of course, just seen her all day at school. If I had gotten to school early enough, I would have sat on the steps with Wiley and seen her coming along Main Street with her little brother Bobby. I saw her in the schoolyard at lunch with Agnes and watched the two of them talk as Agnes put her books in her saddlebags before swinging her leg over the saddle and heading home. When I saw her in the store, I made excuses to talk to her, asked her about where to find something, asked her if she liked working for her father.

"Daddy likes it when I help out, and I don't mind. I learn a lot about how to run the store. Maybe I'll run it myself someday."

I thought her father probably liked having her help him in the store. It also gave him a chance to keep an eye on Annie and keep track of her friends, too.

The Glory post office was part of the store building. On the right wall near the front of the store, a doorway with a few steps led down to the little post office. At the bottom of the steps was a whole wall of little brass mailboxes with windows in the doors that showed the box number. You could go into the post office from the outside, too, but a lot of folks seemed to like going in through the store, stopping to talk with Annie's father before checking their mail. On the front side of the building, around the corner from the mailboxes, the main entrance led to a counter with a window where you could buy stamps and mail letters and packages. A lady named Pearl ran the post office. She was a sturdy woman, with wire-rimmed glasses and steel gray hair tied up in a bun. Annie told me, "If you want to know anything about anybody in Glory, Pearl's the one to ask." A lot of talk went across her counter, and she pretty much kept tabs on everyone in town. "Between her and Sully, they don't miss much."

After a few of these stops at the store for Hal, I found myself stopping by after school even when Hal hadn't asked me to pick anything up. Before school started, Hal had bought me some new things from the "Monkey Wards" catalog, as he called it, and I was still in my school clothes when I stopped in at Sadler's, so I hoped I was presentable.

There was always a lot to do there, and sometimes if there was something I could help out with, I'd jump in without being asked. I helped Annie carry boxes from the storeroom in back and even helped her stock the shelves, although she always had to tell me where things went. Everything had to be just right to please her father. "Be sure to stack the cans on the shelves with the label facing out. Daddy likes everything just so." When she was working in the store, Annie always wore pants, and she usually had Mr. Sadler's turkey feather duster stuck in her back pocket. I thought those tailfeathers were kind of cute. We used the duster to clean the cans and cartons when we put them out and to keep the stuff (Annie called it the "merchandise") that was already on the shelves clean as a whistle. "'There's no room for dirt in my store,' Daddy says."

Sometimes, when it was slow in the store, we sat out back on a little wooden bench there, drinking sodas from the bottle. It was nice sitting with Annie. Boys like Wiley and me were all knuckles and elbows and Adam's apples that bobbed up and down when we talked. Annie was soft in all the right places and always smelled clean like Palmolive soap.

I wondered if she knew how pretty she was. Mostly we talked about school and pretty unimportant stuff, but sometimes we just sat there. Most people seemed uncomfortable with each other if there wasn't anything to talk about. I was like that myself around other people, but it wasn't like that with Annie. I always felt good just being there with her–even when we just sat there without talking.

After a while, I became a regular customer of sorts, one who seldom bought anything, but showed up pretty regularly. Annie's father got used to me, I guess, and when he saw me coming in the door, he'd look up from what he was doing and say, "Hey Justin," and then tell me, "Annie's in the storeroom," or some other place, then return to his work, leaving me to find her on my own. Sometimes, he'd say "Annie's upstairs, helping her mother with dinner," or "She's helping her brother with his homework." That didn't happen too often, but I was always disappointed when it did. If Annie wasn't there, I'd just visit with Mr. Sadler for a bit. He was nice to me, but it made me uneasy without anything much to talk about beside the weather or the news I'd heard on the radio, so I usually didn't stay too long.

Sometimes I helped Waters pick apples after school if there was time before it got dark, and I usually had time to work with him on the weekends. The old trees had taken to the pruning and were putting out a fair number of apples. Waters said they would even be better next year.

One Saturday after I had checked on the cows, I looked up toward Waters' cabin and saw him fussing around outside his apple house, so I walked up to see if he needed any help.

"Not really," he said, "but you can hang around and watch if you want."

"Watch what? What are you doing?"

Waters looked up at me with a funny expression on his face. "I'm fixin' to make up some applejack."

"What's applejack?" I asked.

"It's just apple cider with a kick."

"A kick?"

"Yeah, you know, hard cider—with alcohol in it."

"Really? You know how to do that?"

"Yeah, really." There were some wooden apple boxes stacked against the wall of the apple house. Waters stood two of them on end, sat down on one, and patted the other with his hand. I sat down on the other box.

"Listen, Justin, you been knowin' me a long time now, right? What kind of man you think I am?"I thought about Waters and Daddy, how Daddy said Waters was the only man he ever really trusted. I thought about how Waters treated Momma and me after Daddy died. I thought about how he was with me, how he taught me to drive the Model A. "I think you're a good man," I said.

"Well, thanks for that, but people not always what they seem to be. A long time ago, now, things were different. Before this Depression and all hit the country. Times were pretty good for a lot of people. Some had a lot of money. People like your daddy and me didn't have none. Folks like me hardly ever had money, even then. And your daddy was just a boy, working for shares on a hardscrabble farm. I worked on another farm just down the road from where he was. We got this idea to make us some money, maybe get out of that place before we worked ourselves down to the bone. The temperance people got the country all riled up about Demon Rum, and they passed laws that made alcohol illegal. People still wanted to drink, of course. Lot of them people that voted for Prohibition were still drinking on the sly. It was just popular to vote for the dry laws. Anyway, your daddy and me got the idea that we could maybe take advantage of people's wants and make us some money, too. So we started making whiskey. Got good enough at it that we had a regular business built up, with regular customers and all." He turned and looked at me. "That surprise you?"

"I guess so," I said. I'd never imagined Daddy or Waters doing anything like that—illegal, I mean. They always just worked so hard and everything. I didn't know what to think.

"One time you remember you asked me what my other name was? Not just Waters?"

"Yeah, sure. You said you had one, but you never told me what it was. You just said Waters was good enough."

"That's right. Well, my real name's Leroy—was my daddy's name. But after we started making liquor, people took to calling me "Still," 'cause I was good at making whiskey. Still Waters—that's the name that stuck. After a while that's all they called me, made jokes about that name. People would drive up, ask me was I Still Waters. 'Who else would I be?' I'd say. Got tired of all that after a while.

"After a couple years, the law started moving in on us, busting up other people's stills and hauling them off to jail sometimes. Your daddy and me didn't plan on going to jail so other people could drink whiskey. We could find another line of work. A lot of folks were heading out to California. Still are. Supposed to be a lot of work for folks out here. So we bought an old Model T truck with some of the money we had saved and worked our way out here, too. But I was tired of being Still Waters. I been just Waters ever since we got here.

"Even when he tries, a man slips up sometime. But I'm trying to be a good man. Your daddy was a good man, too. He the only man treated me like we were the same color.

Everybody else see my black skin and get nervous or angry, one. Cutting timber was good work, honest work. Raising apples and making cider be good work, too. But a lotta people don't just like apples for eating or pies or applesauce or apple butter or any of the other things can be made with them. They know you can make liquor out of apples. Shoot— you can make liquor out of most anything. But you can make hard cider or applejack from apples real easy. Say, why do you think old man Weatherby turned loose of the cider press? Hal told him if he could borrow it he'd bring him back some applejack. Hal knows about your daddy and me. Hal doesn't say much, but he knows lots of things. Besides, Hal likes a taste himself now and then.

"Anyway, that's the deal. When the jug is up on that post, there's cider for sale. Regular folks will get cider, but the ones that want it will get the hard stuff. Sully's spreading the word, so I expect there'll be more cars comin' down the road from time to time. Hope this don't change your opinion 'bout me."

"I don't suppose it will," I said. "I just didn't know any of that stuff about you and Daddy and the whiskey and all. I guess I just need time to think about it."

Waters put his arm around my shoulder. "You go ahead and think on it. But you growin' up, and one part of growin' up is finding out that things aren't like you thought they were when you were little. Your eyes wider open than they were, and you seein' things in a whole new way. Sometimes what you see make you unhappy, 'cause it make it seem like the world a bad place. You just seein' that misery for the first time, and it look pretty bad. But after a while you see the joy amongst the misery, and that joy make life worth living. You keep looking for the joy you find around you, and the misery keep to the shadows."

Waters showed me how he made the hard cider and turned it into applejack. He said it wouldn't turn unless you put a "mother" in it to start it working. He made a batch of cider and put it in one of the barrels he found, then added yeast and sugar to it and covered the open end of the barrel with cheesecloth and let it "work." Waters told me the cider would turn "hard" after a while. It would have alcohol in it, but it wouldn't have as much "kick" as most people were looking for. To turn it into applejack, he'd wait until it started to freeze outside overnight, and then he'd go out each morning and take out the water that froze on top of the barrel. That would make for more alcohol in the cider—what people called applejack. Then all he had to do was drain the cider out without stirring up the sludge that settled in the bottom of the barrel. He could put it up in jugs and make everybody happy.

I didn't know how happy everybody was going to be, but I finally understood why Hal was willing to ask Mr. Weatherby to borrow the cider press and why Mr. Weatherby was so anxious to let him have it. I thought I'd just stick to helping pick the apples and learn to make applesauce.

17

By the end of October, most all of the apples had been picked and stored in boxes and stacked in the apple house. Waters had made more cider and applejack, and traffic began to pick up on the Glory Road. Folks would drive up, then stop when they saw that cider jug on the post. Then they'd look up the hill, get out, and start walking up the path to Waters' cabin. A while later they'd come down the hill with a jug or two, or maybe a box of apples. Sometimes Waters would help them carry their stuff down the hill to the car. Apparently he was right about Sully's word-of-mouth advertising. The man could have sold milk to cows. I think he even delivered a few jugs or boxes to people on his route. I didn't know why he was so helpful, until I figured out he was probably getting a jug or two himself.

Along about the first week in November, Uncle Hal was bustling about the house, looking like he was getting ready to go somewhere. It was a Sunday afternoon, and I asked him where he was going.

"Just taking some cider and some apples down to the Weatherbys."

"Can I go with you?"

"I suppose so. You can help me load the things in the car." There was a box of apples and two jugs of cider sitting on the porch when I went out front. I waited while he got his hat and walked to the barn and brought the Model A in front of the house. I put the box on the back seat and set the jugs on the floor before climbing in the front.

I had been asking about having Wiley out to the

ranch, and I figured maybe I could bring it up again. Uncle Hal had said it was okay with him. I told him Mrs. Travers insisted on meeting him before she would let Wiley come out and spend the night. Uncle Hal had said it was okay with him if Wiley came out, but he had never cleared it with Wiley's mother. When we were about halfway to the Weatherbys, I asked him, "Do you think we could go on into town after we leave the Weatherbys and talk to Mrs. Travers about Wiley staying overnight at the ranch? You said you would, but you never did. Couldn't we talk to her this afternoon?"

"I suppose so. You won't ever let me have any peace if I don't, will you?"

"Wiley's my best friend. It'd be nice to see him sometime besides at school."

"Maybe so. You don't really know who your friends are. Sometimes people turn out to be different than you think. But we'll go talk to his mother if you like."

When we pulled in at the Weatherby place, Uncle Hal said, "There's a sack in the back by the apples. Whyn't you make up a nice bag of apples to take to Mrs. Travers? Folks like it when you don't show up empty-handed. Pick out some nice ones. Mr. Weatherby don't care as much about the apples as he does about that cider. Mrs. Weatherby will just figure the box settled some on the way over."

I think we were still calling it "cider" when we got out of the car. He carried the jugs over to the front porch while I struggled along behind him with the box of apples. Old man Weatherby was sitting by himself with his cane draped over the arm of his chair.

"Just set it down in the corner over there, will you? The apples, too. Be just fine right there."

"Got some nice apples there. Make some fine pies. Make good applesauce, too," Hal said, setting the jugs down on the porch.

"Yeah. The wife can do all that if she likes. Be good to have a nice slice of pie after supper. How's the cider?"

I knew what Mr. Weatherby was asking. They were talking in riddles out of respect for my "tenderness," but I thought the whole thing was pretty silly.

"It's a bit 'tart,'" Uncle Hal said, playing along, "But it goes down pretty good. You'll like it, I think."

"I expect I will. I'll give 'er a try."

The way he kept looking at those jugs, I "expected" he could hardly wait till we left to try it, but I didn't say anything. After a little more talking, Mr. Weatherby thanked Uncle Hal again, and we got back in the car and drove on into town.

Wiley was sitting on the front porch when we pulled up to his house. I got out of the car as he walked over to us.

"Hey, Justin."

"Hey. Say–we just stopped by to ask your ma if you could come out to the ranch. This here's my Uncle Hal. I know your ma wants to meet him before she says it's okay."

"She's in the kitchen. I'll tell her you're here."

He went into the house while Hal got out and I fetched the sack of apples from the back and followed Uncle Hal up to the door. We had hardly made it up the steps when the door opened, and Wiley and his mother stood there smiling at us. Mrs. Travers said, "You must be Justin's uncle."

"Name's Harold Brennan, ma'am. Most folks call me Hal. I'm pleased to meet you. Justin's told me how kind you've been to him."

"I'm pleased to meet you, too, Mr. Brennan. I'm Mary Travers. Please come in."

We all went inside. Mrs. Travers led us into the front parlor, where we all took our seats.

I perched on the edge of the settee with Uncle Hal. "We brought you some apples," I said, holding up the bag.

"Why, thank you, Justin. That was very thoughtful of you. Wiley, can you take these into the kitchen? Maybe we could have apple pie when you come to lunch on Wednesday, Justin. How would you like that?"

"That would be fine, ma'am. But you don't have to go to any trouble."

"It's no trouble at all," she said, smiling. "Wiley likes pie, too."

"Is there a Mr. Travers, ma'am?" Uncle Hal asked.

"Yes, but I'm afraid he's not here at the moment. He's working at the Tyler place down the road a ways. He's a farrier, travels to other folks' places, shoeing horses, that sort of thing. I know it's Sunday and all, but nowadays it's hard to get work, and he has to take what he can find."

"I understand, ma'am. Times are tough. Folks are lucky to find whatever work they can."

"So true. But anyway, it's good to meet you. Justin said he would like to invite Wiley to stay at your ranch over the weekend sometime. I hope you don't mind. I wanted to meet Justin's folks, make sure it was all right if Wiley came to visit."

"Perfectly fine, Mrs. Travers. I can see why you'd feel that way, not knowing anything about us. I'm Justin's uncle, great-uncle actually. His mother, Molly, is my niece. She's away at the moment, and Justin's staying with me."

I had never seen Uncle Hal like this before. He was all charm and manners. Laying it on a little too thick, I thought. "His mother's 'away' at the moment." What was that supposed to mean? But I really wanted Wiley to come out to the ranch, so I kept my mouth shut. Sometimes it was hard to figure out the things grownups did.

Anyway, by the end of our visit, Wiley's mother and Uncle Hal agreed that Wiley could come home with me after school on Friday. Hal explained that I drove to school, said I had lots of practice by now, and said that he would see that Wiley got back in time for school on Monday.

On the way home, I asked why Uncle Hal hadn't said anything about Waters and how he lived with us on the ranch.

"I didn't think it was important," was all he said.

18

Friday seemed a long way off, but Mr. Phillips kept us busy. He always gave us spelling tests on Monday. He had divided us into four groups, and each group had a different test. Wiley and me were in the same group, along with Agnes Wheelock and Annie Sadler. Agnes still acted like she was pretty pleased with herself, but it was easy to tell Wiley liked her a lot. I didn't know if Agnes knew. She did seem pretty stuck on her herself.

Annie was all right, though. She didn't call attention to herself in class the way Agnes did, but she always had my attention. She seemed kind of shy, didn't talk any more than I did, but I knew by now how smart she was. I kept quiet so I wouldn't embarrass myself in front of her or the class, either one. We usually let Agnes do most of the talking, unless Mr. Phillips called on us directly.

Since Jesse and Curt were so much older, he made them a group of their own, but since they hadn't spent much time in school, he often had them sit in with the younger kids for reading and arithmetic. Sometimes he let them sit in with our group, which made me and Wiley pretty jumpy. Agnes had to be careful not to make Jesse look dumb, and Wiley had to try not to give too much attention to Agnes. I just tried to keep up with Mr. Phillips without getting the stinkeye from Jesse and Curt, who were going to be trouble sooner or later.

Mr. Phillips said the words out loud and gave us time to write them down. Most of us studied the lists Mr. Phillips gave out on Friday, but Jesse and Curt hardly ever did. They never learned the habit of studying. I hadn't spent enough time in school to learn any habits, but I was trying to do what Mr. Phillips asked. He had been fair enough so far and I wanted to show him I was making progress.

Sometimes Jesse and Curt would try to copy off one of our papers, but we tried not to let them do it. I think Mr. Phillips suspected what was going on, but he hadn't said anything about it yet. Sometimes I thought he felt a little sorry for Jesse and Curt, since they were so much older and seemed out of place most of the time.

Anyway, Mr. Phillips had us clear our table, and then he passed out paper for the spelling tests. We wrote our names at the top and numbered from one to ten down the left side along the margin. Then he read off the words, and we wrote them down. He said each word, used it in a sentence, and then repeated it one more time before moving on to the next word. Wiley and me had studied together for a few minutes before school started, so we were okay, but Jesse and Curt must not have studied, 'cause they were looking around at our papers. I thought I could feel Jesse's breath on my neck. Wiley must have felt something, too, because he glanced over toward Jesse and told him to turn around.

Mr. Phillips looked at Wiley and said, "Do you have a question, Mr. Travers? If so, please ask me, not Mr. Wheelock."

Wiley snapped, "I just told him to keep his eyes on his own paper. He's always trying to copy off our papers."

"Why would I want to copy off you?" Jesse said, pushing his chair back from the table.

Mr. Phillips said, "That's quite enough of that." And then he did something he had never done before. He had us stand up, and then he called on each of us one at a time and made us spell one of the words from the list out loud. He went around the table twice, and every time he got to Jesse and Curt, they didn't know the words. Wiley and Agnes got all of theirs right, but Annie and I each missed one. When Mr. Phillips moved on to the younger kids, I thought everything was okay, but when I saw Jesse giving Wiley a mean look, I wasn't too sure.

At lunchtime, Agnes left the group of girls she was sitting with and came over to where Wiley and me were sitting on our favorite bench. She looked at Wiley and said, "I know Jesse probably was looking at your paper like you said, but you need to watch out for him. He knows he isn't very good at school, but he doesn't like it if he's made to look bad in front of the class."

"Why are you telling me all this?" Wiley said.

"I just don't want anything bad to happen to you," Agnes said, and then she turned away and walked back to the other girls.

"I think she likes you," I said.

After lunch, Mr. Phillips started an arithmetic lesson on subtraction. I didn't really know that word, but I soon realized he was talking about what Miss Gravy called "take aways." I could hear her again saying, "Nine take away five leaves how many?" I knew how to do that okay when the numbers were small, and I could figure it out in my head. When the numbers were bigger, and I had to do it on paper, it seemed a lot harder.

Mr. Phillips tried to explain it to us in his own way. He said, "Pretend you've got one hundred and twenty-three horses on your farm and your neighbor wants to buy thirty-nine of them." He turned and wheeled the chalkboard in front of the class. He wrote the numbers on the chalkboard, putting the bigger number on top. He drew a line under the numbers.

Amos Weatherby said, "Ain't nobody 'round here got that many horses," and then looked around to see if anybody thought that was funny.

There were a few giggles, but Mr. Phillips cleared his throat, and continued. "Let's look at this a different way," he said. He reached up near the top of the chalkboard and pulled down a chart that unrolled like a window shade. It had a picture of a street with three houses on it. Each house had a tree beside it and a red chimney on top. Each house had a little pocket on the door, and Mr. Phillips took some cards from his desk and sorted through them. They all had large numbers on them. He put a big 1 on the first door, a 2 on the second door, and a 3 on the last door.

"This is a little neighborhood where everyone knows each other. Mrs. Brown lives in the house on the left, Mrs. Jones lives in the middle, and Mrs. Smith lives in the house on the right." He paused and wrote the name over each house. They're good friends, like to help one another out if they can." He pointed to the house on the right. "Mrs. Smith is kind of poor. She never has more than nine things at a time and often needs her neighbors' help. Next door is Mrs. Jones. She has more than Mrs. Smith, always buys things ten at a time, so she's happy to help. But sometimes even Mrs. Jones finds herself a little short and has to get help from Mrs. Brown who always buys things by the hundred."

"That lady must be rich," Amos said.

Mr. Phillips was not to be stopped. He pointed to the numbers he had written on the board earlier. "We want to subtract 39 from 123, but if we try to take 9 away from 3, we can't. Why not?"

"Nine is more than three," David Sykes shouted.

"That's correct. In our model, if we ask Mrs. Smith to

gives us nine from the three she has, she can't do it. So what will she do? She wants to help."

Amos said, "She can go next door to Mrs. Jones!"

"That's right," Mr. Phillips said. "But remember, Mrs. Jones always has ten of everything, so if Mrs. Smith wants to borrow from Mrs. Jones, she has to borrow ten at a time.

"If she borrows ten from Mrs. Jones and adds them to what she already has, how many does she have now?"

"Thirteen," several kids shouted.

"That's correct," Mr. Phillips said. He crossed out Mrs. Jones' 2 on the board and changed it to a 1. Then he put a 1 next to Mrs. Smith's 3, making it into 13. "Now if we take nine from thirteen, what are we left with?"

"Four!"

"Let's raise hands to answer–remember?" Mr. Phillips wrote a 4 under the line.

"Now Mrs. Jones only has one of her tens left. Can we take three away from one?"

"No!"

"Hands, please. Who knows what to do now? "

Agnes raised her hand.

"Yes, Miss Wheelock?"

"You have to borrow the one from Mrs. Brown, make Mrs. Jones' one into eleven, and take away three, leaving eight. The answer is eighty-four."

That Agnes certainly wasn't going to hide her light under a bushel.

"Thank you, Miss Wheelock. That's a little more help than I was looking for, but you're correct, of course.

"Look, everyone, we've only known one another for a few weeks now. As we continue, the groups you're in will change as I learn more about what you already know. Some of you will undoubtedly be helping each other to learn. Be patient a while longer."

I thought Agnes was just showing off, but Mr. Phillips wasn't offended at all. In fact, he seemed to act like Agnes could be helpful in class. We'd just have to wait and see, I supposed, but I wasn't so sure. I didn't envy Mr. Phillips.

On Wednesday, Wiley and me went to his house for lunch as usual. We ate in the kitchen now, which helped me relax a little since I didn't have to fret so much about breaking something or spilling on the carpet. I was right at home in the kitchen with the plain table and the well-worn oilcloth covering it. Mrs. Travers had baked an apple pie like she said she would, and it was still warm when we got there for lunch. After we ate our usual lunch, we each had a big slice of pie before heading back to school. I hadn't eaten anything that good since Momma went away. It made me feel nice, but kind of sad at the same time.

When we got back to the school, the other kids were still out in the schoolyard. As we walked toward the steps, Wiley looked over to where Agnes was sitting with her friends. She looked up just then and saw us. Wiley waved at her, and she waved back, but hers was a cautious, almost secret wave that her friends probably didn't even notice. When we got to the porch steps, Jesse and Curt were sitting there, slouching. They gave Wiley a look. Mr. Phillips came out on the porch about then and rang the bell, and we all filed into class behind him.

When Friday finally came, I was glad. Wiley was finally going to come out to the ranch, and we could both stop looking over our shoulders for Jesse and Curt. Having someone my own age to go around with would be a welcome change.

After school, we stopped by Wiley's to pick up some of his things for the weekend. Wiley's mother came out on the porch to wave good-bye to us. She handed me a fresh-baked loaf of bread wrapped in a towel to take with us. I thanked her, and Wiley and me got into the car. I tried to be especially careful when we took off, and she stood on the porch watching us drive away. I didn't want her to think she'd just sent Wiley off with a madman or anything.

As we rolled along on the Glory Road, Wiley asked me where I'd learned to drive. I told him about Waters and how he'd been my daddy's friend before he got killed, how he'd taught me to drive so I could go to school in town. Wiley said they had a car, an old Model T pickup his father used to travel to folks' places to do his horseshoeing and all. He said his pa had said he would teach him to drive some time, but he hadn't gotten around to it yet.

When we got to the ranch, it was near dinnertime and starting to get dark. As eager as I was to show Wiley around, that would have to wait. We went inside and washed up. Uncle Hal still wasn't much for cooking, but he had made a pot roast with carrots and onions and potatoes, all cooked together. We sopped up the gravy with big slices of the bread that Wiley's mother made, and it was a fine meal, a little bit special because we had company.

After dinner, we washed up the dishes and went into the front room. Uncle Hal was stirring up the coals in the fireplace, putting on more wood. I asked him if I could play the piano for Wiley and was surprised when he said, "I suppose so." He didn't even ask me to play that *Rose of Tralee* that he liked so much.

Wiley sat on the bench with me, and I showed him how the piano worked. We took turns pumping the pedals, playing four or five songs before Uncle Hal said that was enough for one evening. By then, both of us had worked up a sweat and were about ready to quit anyway. We put the piano rolls back in the cabinet and went to my room.

I showed Wiley my crystal set, and we listened to *Fibber McGee and Molly*. I kind of liked it because Molly's name was the same as Momma's, but they were nothing like each other, of course. We sat on the floor, each of us listening with one of the headphone earpieces.

Molly was bitten by the "new car bug" and was trying to get McGee to trade in their old car. She called it an "antiquated egg beater," and said it "pumped more oil than the Rockefellers." McGee said she was trying to make him go "high hat." He was a Democrat, and he wanted to drive a Democratic car. She said she didn't care if it was Democratic or Republican, but she knew they'd never get a third party to ride in it. The radio audience really liked that one. It was a funny show, as usual, and Wiley and me laughed a lot. When it was over, we got ready for bed. Since he was company, I let Wiley have the bed, and I slept on the floor. I didn't really mind. It was nice to have some company.

19

The next morning, after breakfast, we went out to the barn, broke open a bale of hay and tossed a few forkfuls over the fence to the cows. They'd made their trip back to the Weatherby's for breeding one day while I was at school and were going to be having their calves early next summer. Uncle Hal didn't ask my opinion when he decided to do something. Most of the time I was just there in the house with him, like the furniture. It wasn't like he never talked to me, but he didn't seem to worry much about what I was thinking. Waters was different. He listened to me like what I said mattered, even if it didn't amount to much. Uncle Hal probably didn't even think about me when he took the cows back to the Weatherby's. It was okay for me to drive twenty miles every day to learn to spell and do long division, but he didn't think I was old enough to learn some things every farm boy my age already knew.

After we left the barn, we walked down the road and turned up the path to Waters' cabin. When we got to the apple house, I showed Wiley around, told him how I had helped Waters dig out the hillside and saw up the logs that Waters split to frame the roof. Then we went inside to take a look. Waters had stacked the filled apple boxes in long rows from end to end in the apple house, with just enough space in between for a person to walk and take down the boxes as they were needed. He had sorted them by the different types of apples they had in them. Along one wall, he had lined up the big crocks filled with cider and the barrels he had used for the applejack. At first the barrels had been outside under the roof overhang. When the weather cooled and there was a good hard freeze, Waters had gone out each morning and taken off the ice on top until the barrels were only a little more than half full. Then he had drained the cider out through the spigot near the bottom of the barrel, just above the sludge. He put it up in the syrup jugs from the soda fountain. Most of the applejack was gone by now, sold to the new travelers on the Glory Road and given away to folks like Mr. Weatherby and Sully and Uncle Hal, who had helped his business along. People still came up the road now and then, but they only bought apples and the regular cider Waters had left.

After I showed Wiley around the apple house, we hiked up the hill to the orchard behind Waters' cabin. We saw him up ahead of us working on his "All-American" tree. When we got closer, Waters saw us, and stepped down from the ladder he was standing on.

"Morning, Justin. Who's that you got with you?"

"This is Wiley, my friend from school. He came home with me last night. He's going to stay over till Monday."

"Nice to meet you," Waters said, extending his hand to Wiley.

Wiley hesitated a little, then stepped forward and shook hands. "Nice to meet you, too," he said. "Justin said you were the one taught him to drive."

"That's right. Needed to know how so he could get to school. How's he doing? He scare you yet?"

"No," Wiley said, "He drives real good. I wish Pa would teach me. Always says he will, but he hasn't yet."

"Wiley's daddy's a farrier, travels all around shoeing horses and stuff."

"That be good work—important, too. Horse come up lame, get hoof trouble, he can't work. Your daddy needed where he go. He get around to teachin' you to drive. Maybe one day he show you how to take care of the horses, too. Be a good thing to learn."

I asked Waters what he was doing with the old crabapple tree. He reminded me that he had only cut back part of the tree last year because it would have been too hard on it. So this year he was cutting back on the rest of the tree. He would put new grafts on the rest of the limbs this spring. He showed Wiley where we had put the grafts on last year and told how most of them had taken and grown out over the summer.

"Maybe next year we might get a few apples on those grafts that took this year. Have to wait and see. But one day, expect to see all colors of apples on the 'All-American' here."

Waters reminded me that pretty soon he could use a little help cutting the scions for the grafting next spring. He said we had started on the All-American together, and we should see it through together. "Give us something to talk about when we're old," he said, laughing.

After we talked a bit more, Wiley and me said good-bye and started back down the path to the road. "What'd you think of Waters?" I asked.

Wiley stopped walking and looked at me. The expression on his face reminded me of how he looked in class when Mr. Phillips asked him a question and he didn't know the answer. "How come you never said he was a Negro?"

It had never even crossed my mind that Wiley would feel strange meeting Waters. I guess I had expected more from Wiley. I should have known better.

"He's just Waters to me, I guess. Does it make any difference?"

"I don't suppose it does, only I ain't ever met one before. Not to talk to, I mean."

" 'I ain't ever met one' sounds like you're talking about

a thing, not a person. Waters is as much a man as anybody you see on the street in Glory–maybe more. You hear people call folks like Waters all kinda names. Call 'em niggers, and all kinda mean names like that. I've known Waters my whole life. He was my daddy's partner, worked with him every day until he got killed. Daddy said Waters was the only man he ever really trusted. Waters is a good man, looked after Momma and me when Daddy died. Talks to me like I'm a whole person, not just a kid, like most grownups do. I think most people never really get to know each other, so they go around afraid of each other all the time. I bet there are lots of folks his color who are just as mean and hateful as the mean and hateful white folks we know already, but Waters isn't like them. Waters is just like the good folks you already know."

"I didn't mean anything by what I said. I'm sorry if you thought I was being hurtful. I ain't ever heard you say that much all at one time. I guess I hit a nerve or something."

"It's okay, Wiley. I shouldn't have jumped all over you. It's just that Waters has been good to me, helps me figure out who I am. It would be a stretch to think you'd see all that the first time you meet someone."

20

That afternoon I asked Uncle Hal if we could use the car for a while. I wanted to show Wiley that abandoned railroad track and the old mine that Waters and I had found.

"I suppose," he said. "Just don't go tearin' ass up and down the road. That car's the only thing keeping you in school. Take care of it."

I told him we'd be careful and said we'd come back before it got dark. Wiley and me went out to the barn, started up the car, and headed back down the road. When we got to where the railroad track crossed the road, I turned off onto the little overgrown dirt path that ran up to the mine. I parked there, and we hiked the rest of the way.

Uncle Hal didn't seem to know about Waters saying we should keep away from the old mine. He only seemed worried that I might damage the car. I didn't think Hal had to worry about me wrecking the car, but I felt a little guilty about going against what Waters had said. I decided it was one of those warnings parents give their kids to keep them out of trouble, knowing that they'll probably do it anyway. Besides, there wasn't that much to do, and I wanted Wiley to have a good time.

The path to the mine was littered with bits of broken glass that glittered in the sunlight, rusted tin cans, and lengths of rusty wire rope. Rotting wooden ties with rusty iron spikes sticking out of them were piled higgledy-piggledy here and there. Insects buzzed in that high-pitched way that seems loud in your ears, and grasshoppers sprang up as we made our way through the tall weeds that had grown up along the path. A kingsnake slithered out of his sunspot ahead of us, and a lizard skittered under the rock he'd been sunning himself on.

At the mine, we clomped around, looking the place over. We walked over to the hoist house where the head frame stuck up in the air. We looked through a hole in the wall and tossed some rocks down the shaft, trying to figure how deep it was. It was hard to tell, but we thought we could hear it splash when the rocks hit the bottom.

"How'd you find this place?" Wiley asked.

"Waters and me found it when I was practicing driving. We stopped here to turn around one time, and we walked up the railroad track to see where it went."

We poked around, looking into the old buildings. Most of them had rusty tin roofs that sagged inward, and some of them leaned a little, like they were about to fall over. Most of the windowpanes were broken, and the doors hung open, sagging from their own weight. We weren't the only ones who had been here looking around. A breeze came up and stirred the trees along the path, and some of the buildings creaked and groaned like old man Weatherby when he got up out of that wicker chair. We looked inside each one, hoping to find something interesting, but most of them were pretty much empty, with just some rubbish lying around on the floor. Here and there we found a piece of equipment, big iron pulleys and such, too heavy to carry away. An old ore cart sat on rusted rails. Wiley gave it a push, but it wouldn't budge.

One of the buildings was set into the hillside, with a lower level underneath the main one. The lower level looked like it had been a workshop of some kind. It had a forge in the center of the floor, and there was a big tin chimney poking through the outside wall that went clear to the top of the roof over the main floor above us. There was an old

Model T dump truck inside. Someone had cranked the bed open, and it looked like that was the only thing holding up the floor above. The floor underneath the truck sagged from its weight, too. It looked like the kind of place Waters had warned me about, but it was just too interesting to pass up. Wiley immediately climbed into the cab of the old truck, pretending to drive as he gripped the big wooden steering wheel.

"We better get out of here, Wiley. That whole floor's about ready to fall in. Only thing holding it up is that truck bed."

"In a minute. It ain't gonna fall in today. It's probably been like this for ages."

He was getting carried away, I could tell. He started hopping up and down on the seat and twisting the wheel back and forth. Without any warning, the board floor under the front wheel gave a big crack, and the wheel sank through a hole that appeared in the floor. When that happened, the whole truck tilted some, and there was a big noise from the floor above. Wiley jumped out of the cab like he'd just sat on a nail, and we headed for the door. We got out fine, and after some creaks and groans, the building settled. Apparently the old truck was still doing its job. There were some tools lying around and some old bottles half-buried in the rubbish strewn on the floor. Wiley poked around in the mess with a stick.

"Hey, look at this."

He held up an interesting-looking bottle that had started to turn purple. "Look, here's another one." He brought the bottles over to show me. "What'd you find.?"

I was looking at a rusty iron candleholder that had been driven into the framing on one wall. It looked handmade, with one end bent and twisted around to make a finger hold. I wiggled it back and forth till it came loose in my hand. The other end had been made sharp to stick into the wall. "Some kind of candleholder, I think. See, there's a socket on top with some wax in it."

In one of the other buildings we could see an old iron bed frame through the door, but the floor was caving in, so we stayed outside. A metal tank with streaks of rust running down its sides stood on legs behind the building, and we found some more cables and pulleys heaped in a pile beside it. We spent an hour or more looking around the place. It was interesting trying to figure out what all the things we saw were used for. I had kept the rusty candleholder, and Wiley held onto the purple bottles he had found.

After we had looked in most of the buildings, I began to worry a little about being gone so long. If we got back in time for me to do my chores before dinner, I didn't expect any trouble. Wiley wanted to keep looking, but I managed to pry him away before anything else collapsed. We walked back to the car and headed home with our treasures.

After dinner that night, Wiley and me showed Hal what we had found at the mine. We left out a few details, like the near collapse of that building and Waters' notion that going there wasn't a good idea in the first place. He said the candleholder was the kind miners used to use in the old days, before they had the more reliable kerosene lanterns. It was made like it was with the point on one end so it could be pounded into one of the timbers in the mineshaft.

"Those bottles are old patent medicine bottles. People used to buy all kinds of strange medicines for their ailments. A lot of them were mostly alcohol. Those quack remedies might not have cured what ailed the folks that bought 'em, but they sure made 'em feel better. It was manganese in the glass that made the old bottles turn color. Before the war they used manganese when they made the glass. That's one way to tell how old they are."

Hal knew about a lot of things, but most of the time he didn't say much. Once he got going, though, sometimes he came out with some pretty interesting ideas.

When we got up the next morning, it was raining. It wasn't a gullywasher or anything, but it kind of put the squash on hiking around outdoors. I wanted to take Wiley down to the creek where Waters and I had gone fishing last summer, but that was out for sure.

After breakfast, we sat on the floor in front of the fireplace and played a few games of checkers. Wiley mostly beat me, but I managed to win a couple of games. After a while, we got tired of checkers and went out on the front porch. The rain had slacked off, so we put on our jackets and headed down to the barn.

Sometimes I just went down to the barn when I had nothing else to do. I liked the way it smelled, how it was big and dark inside. It was always cooler in the barn in the summer, and the sun came in through gaps in the walls and made interesting shapes on the floor. The barn was the last stop for anything that got used up or went out of fashion, and there were lots of interesting things to see. There was even a little room in the back where Hal reloaded the shells for his guns. It had a lock on the door, and I wasn't allowed to go in there by myself. I had peeked through a crack in the door, but I couldn't see much, just part of what looked like a workbench on the far wall, a machine with a handle sticking up at the top clamped to the edge. There were some tins and cardboard boxes lined up against the wall at the back and a calendar on the wall with a half-naked lady over a tablet with the days of the month. I think there might've been more of those calendars on that wall, but I could only see so much through that crack, no matter how hard I tried.

Wiley and me poked around in the barn, looking at the horse collars and cow kickers and the hay hooks and baling twine and bee smokers and the jars of bag balm and other fascinating stuff that had collected in the barn. Finally, we climbed up on the hay bales that were stacked high in the middle part of the barn and sat for a while, looking down over the whole place. There was a floor to the hayloft just below the big doors that opened out near the peak of the roof. A wooden ladder was built onto the wall so you could reach that floor without having to climb on the hay. We got down from the pile and climbed up the ladder to the loft. We opened those doors and stood there for a while, looking out at the road below and the countryside further off. We could see the willows along the creek and the hills on the other side of it with their tops disappearing into the fog. Waters' cabin was on one side and Uncle Hal's house was on the other, but the barn cut off our view, so we couldn't see either one. We thought it might be like flying in a plane and looking out the window at the country down below, only maybe not as high.

Up near the peak of the roof, there was a hay trolley that ran along a metal track that hung from the rafters and ran outside above the big doors. The trolley had two pairs of wheels on top that rode along the metal track and a block and tackle that hung from a pair of pulleys on the bottom. The whole contraption was used to load hay into the barn through those doors that we'd been looking out of. When they loaded hay into the barn, the trolley would be rolled out to the end of the track outside and the block and tackle would be lowered to the ground. Some men outside would shove big metal hooks into several bales of hay at a time, making a big bundle. Then they used a horse or a car hooked to the rope to pull the bales of hay up to the open doors, where they would run inside along the metal track near the ceiling. A man inside had a rope he pulled that tripped a catch on those big hooks, and then the hay bales fell inside, and men would grab them with hay hooks, wrestle them around, and stack them.

Hal had bought some hay for his cows from the feed store in town, and I went out to watch them unload the hay and stack it in the barn. Uncle Hal told me I was "too light in the poop" to shuffle the heavy hay bales around, but I grabbed a couple of hay hooks and showed him I had a little Irish elbow grease myself. When the bundled bales reached the middle of the barn, Uncle Hal gave out a loud whistle, Waters pulled the rope, and the bales dropped to the floor, sending up a cloud of hay dust that stuck to our clothes and hair. The three of us scrambled to stack the bales while the men from the feed store pulled the trolley back and put together another load from the truck. It was dirty, sweaty work, but I liked working alongside Waters and Uncle Hal. It was one of the few times we had done something together.

The ends of the rope that went up around the block and tackle were gathered together now and tied off on a hook screwed into the wall by the end doors. If we held onto both ends of the rope at the same time, it was possible to swing out on the rope into the middle of the barn and then swing back to where we stood on the floor of the loft. I explained that to Wiley, but he seemed skeptical about it. I thought he'd probably lost a little of his courage after what happened at the mine.

"What if we can't get back and we're just stuck hanging there in the middle?" He said. "Or what if our hands slip, and we fall off?"

"Then you just have to let go and fall off in the hay." I made it sound like it was no big deal, but the barn didn't really have much hay in it yet, and the hay was a long way down. It was also baled hay, not nearly as soft as loose hay would have been.

"You do it first," Wiley said.

"Okay, just watch." I reached up as high as I could, gathered both ends of the rope in my hands, and wrapped them around my arm. Then I lifted my feet up and swung out into the air, pointing my toes at the other side of the barn. It was pretty scary the first time, but when the rope reached the limit of its swing, I swung back and handed the rope to Wiley as I landed with a thump on the floor of the loft. "Your turn," I told him.

He reached up and grabbed the rope, wrapping it around his arm like I had done. Then he just stood there, looking at me. "Go ahead," I told him. "It's fun. Just push as hard as you can so you'll swing all the way back. Go ahead. I'll catch you."

Wiley looked out over the barn floor below us. Then he took a deep breath and pushed off. He swung out into the air and came back. I grabbed the rope before he let go of it, and he landed with a thump beside me. After he had caught his breath, he said, "Say, that was fun. Let's do it again."

We spent another half hour or so swinging back and forth on the rope. We pretended we were sailors swinging from the yardarms to battle pirates trying to board our ship or just flying through the air like acrobats in a circus. I think our arms were getting tired because one time Wiley stumbled when he tried to take off and just sort of fell off the platform, spinning in the air. He held onto the rope, though, and after pumping his legs as he swung back and forth a few times, he managed to get close enough that I could grab him before he swung back. After that we tied the rope off on the hook again just like we had found it. Then we climbed back down the ladder to the floor again, and walked back to the house for lunch.

21

Monday morning we got up when my Big Ben woke us, and got ready for school. I pulled out all the stops for breakfast. I made us some Cream of Wheat and poured a little syrup on top for flavor. I burned some toast in the frying pan and smeared some store-bought jelly on top. Wiley was polite about it, but knowing the way his ma could cook, I was sure he was used to something better to start his day.

We put on our jackets and grabbed our books, and I made sure to take the lunch I had packed the night before. It was still raining when we ran out to get in the car. I turned on the lights and the wiper, and we headed off to Glory. The Model A had a vacuum wiper, and every time I headed up a little hill and pressed harder on the gas pedal to keep the speed up, the wiper slowed down. Then when we went over the top of the hill, and I let off on the gas, the wiper speeded up. Besides, there was only one wiper, and it only wiped part of the window. It was pretty comical, but it was also hard to see where I was going, so I had to go a lot slower. Driving to school in the winter was not going to be nearly as much fun.

Since it was Monday, we practiced the spelling words on our way to Glory. Wiley read the words to me as we drove along, and I tried to spell them out loud. I kept getting stuck on "reticent." What kind of word was that? I couldn't imagine ever having to use that word. Wiley said it meant shy or reluctant. Well, if it meant shy, why not just say shy and be done with it? I wasn't too sure about reluctant, either, but Wiley said it was another meaning of reticent, kind of like when you didn't want to do something. I couldn't wait to hear what Uncle Hal said when I told him I was reticent about doing my chores. I expected that would go over really big.

By the time we got to school, I had a little better idea of how to spell the words, so I thought I would do pretty well on Mr. Phillips' test. There were no horses tied up outside the school. I guessed Agnes and Jesse decided to stay in out of the rain. I didn't know about Curt. Mr. Phillips was standing under the porch overhang. He had the door open early, and he was standing in the doorway, motioning us to come in out of the rain. We put our coats in the closet and went into the classroom. He must have come in early, 'cause there was a roaring fire in the stove, and the room was almost warm when we went inside.

The rain slacked off in the middle of the morning, and Agnes and her brother trotted up to the school in time for the spelling test. After they hung up their rain-streaked slickers, they were still a little damp around the edges but more or less okay. Agnes' red hair seemed darker when wet, and Wiley whispered to me that he kind of liked the little curl that was plastered to her forehead. Curt never did show up. When Mr. Phillips got around to us, I got all the words right except you-know-what. Wiley was looking pretty pleased with himself, having gotten them all correct for a change. Agnes had gotten a perfect score, too. I didn't see how Jesse did. He just took his paper back and turned it over real quick so no one could see it.

Later that afternoon, when we usually studied history while the little ones read their story books, Mr. Phillips announced that he had something special in mind, and he wanted everyone to pay attention. We all put down our books to listen.

"You probably know," he said, pushing his glasses back on his nose, "that Thanksgiving is coming up in a few weeks. I don't know what the custom is at this school since this is my first year here, but I know that Thanksgiving is a time to think about our blessings and be thankful for them. It is a time to celebrate with family and friends, to be thankful for what we have and for the people we have around us." He paused then, looking at each of us in turn. "I'm proposing that we put on a Thanksgiving pageant. I think it will bring us all a little closer to each other and to your families and their friends. Do all of you know what a pageant is?" He asked.

When no one said anything, Mr. Phillips smiled and said, "It's a kind of a show that we can put on for everyone to see. I'm calling it 'Paths to Glory'. I propose that we all celebrate who we are and how we came to be here. Times are hard just now, and many people think there isn't much to be happy about. But I think we can look into our hearts and be happy about who we are and where we have come from and what brought us here. I think 'Paths to Glory' is a fine name, and I'm sure you will all be proud of yourselves when we're finished."

Mr. Phillips talked about his "pageant" a little while longer, saying we would each have a part to play, and how he would explain more as we got closer to the holiday.

The rain was still holding off when I got back in the Model A that afternoon after school. Mr. Phillips had made us all a little uncomfortable. We all suspected his little "pageant" wasn't going to be as much fun as he thought it was. That part about putting on a show *for everyone to see* had Wiley and me pretty jumpy to say the least. We didn't exactly know what he had in mind, but it didn't sound good to us.

I needed to stop at the filling station to get gas in the car. Before we left the house, Uncle Hal had given me a dollar to fill the tank, so I stopped at the corner and let Al do the honors. I was sitting there, waiting, looking up and down the street while he filled the tank from his antique pump. I looked over at the Snug on the opposite corner across the street. It was the same shabby place I had seen every day as I passed by on Main Street. Uncle Hal had called it a "dive," and said the only people that went there were low types and drifters on their way to nowhere. I suspected Glory must have its share of low types. A place like the Snug couldn't keep its doors open if their business depended on people who were just drifting through town. Even though the radio said the country was full of "gasoline gypsies," there weren't enough people passing through Glory to keep the streets free of tumbleweeds.

While I was thinking all of this over, a man came out of the Snug, leaned his back to the front wall, rolled a cigarette, and set fire to it. He had on a black slouch hat and dirty overalls, and he looked as if he was more than half way on his trip to nowhere. Maybe he'd already been there and was on his way back.

Al finished filling the tank, put the cap on, and wiped it off with his red rag. I wondered if it was the same rag, or if he had a whole bunch of them, and he traded off from time to time. I gave Al my dollar and started the car. As I started down the street, I drove slowly, looking over at the man as he leaned against the wall, smoking. Even though the hat cast a shadow over his face, I could see he had a long scar, running from below his left eye almost to his chin. I remembered what Waters had said that night as we drove away from the mill. When the man looked toward the car, I turned away from him and sped up as I drove past.

22

On the way back to the ranch, I tried to figure out what to do. I wanted to tell somebody about the man in the black hat, but I didn't know who to tell. Waters was the one he had threatened back at the mill, but what would he do about it now? It would just give him something to worry about, and Waters wasn't the worrying kind, at least not so I could tell. I thought about telling Uncle Hal. He was the one who had stepped in and got Waters and Momma and me out of trouble, but what could he do now? He wasn't boss of the woods around here. I couldn't see him riding Shorty into town to run the man out of Glory with his bullwhip. Where was the Lone Ranger and his faithful Indian companion now? What would they have done?

I still hadn't figured out what to do when I got home. I parked in the barn and just sat there for a while, turning it all over in my mind and getting nowhere. Finally, I got out, closed the door to the barn, and walked along the road to the house. I went through the back door into the kitchen. Uncle Hal was stirring something in a pot on the stove.

"Thought we'd have some soup—good on a cold day like this." He looked up at me and put the spoon down on the stove. "What's wrong with you? You look like you've seen a haunt."

I didn't know what to say, so I just told him. "You remember that night at the mill when we left 'cause those men were after Momma and had Waters tied up by the pond?"

"What about it?"

"I stopped to get gas tonight. While Al was putting in the gas, I saw a man come out of that place called the Snug. He had a big scar on the left side of his face, and he was wearing a black hat. He looked like the man Waters told about, the one who had him tied up, about to push him into the pond."

"Are you sure? There's lots of men walking around under black hats."

"I remember seeing him around the cookhouse myself, when we were back there. Hard not to remember someone who looks like that."

"I suppose. He certainly had a look about him. I'd hoped we were done with him."

"Maybe he's passing through town, going somewhere else."

"Maybe so. Maybe not. Probably worth looking into, though."

"You think he's after Waters?"

"I don't know who he's after," Uncle Hal said. "Maybe he's not after anyone. But a man like that has a one-track mind. He probably isn't after Waters. He doesn't like Negroes. That's for sure. Probably a lot of other kinds of people he doesn't like. No, Waters didn't do anything to him. Waters was just there at the wrong time. Man was drunk and all, looking for some kind of scrap to get into.

"If he's after anyone, it's probably me he's after. Remember, I embarrassed him in front of the other men, made him look bad. Hard to forget someone who does that to you. And then the mill closed down soon after we left. I was the foreman. He might think my running off had something to do with the mill closing, even if it didn't. A man that loses face and then loses his job is not likely to forget the one he thinks caused him all that misery. If he's looking for anybody, it's probably me he wants."

"What can we do about it?"

"We're not going to do anything right now. Just wait and see. Maybe he'll move on. Maybe he's not after anybody. You keep an eye out when you're in town. Don't go off by yourself. Be careful."

I drove to school the next morning, as usual. I was on the lookout, but I didn't see Black Hat anywhere. Maybe he had moved on. I certainly hoped so. I had plenty more to worry about. Mr. Phillips continued to drop hints about his pageant idea to us. He said the pageant would be all about Glory, how the town sprang up at the crossroads, how it was a place where people came from all kinds of different places to make something new where nothing had been before. He said it was kind of like America itself.

Man had a lot of imagination, if you asked me. If Glory was somebody's grand plan for the future, it had fizzled out a long time ago. Wasn't anything glorious about this place that I could see. But Mr. Phillips was unstoppable. Every day he had something new to add to his grand design. The whole thing would take place on the stage at the front of the room up where the preacher spoke on the Sundays he was in town.

He'd already had us make a big banner with "Paths to Glory" in red, white, and blue paint, and he'd hung it on the wall at the back of the stage. It had silver stars surrounding the words, and it did look pretty good, even if some of the paint had run a little. But he had gotten Jesse and Curt to put it up right away so we could look at it every day and be "inspired," he said. He'd told Tommy, Alice, and Aaron, the littlest kids, that they would be little pioneers. Mrs. Potts, the lady that played the piano at church, would play "America, the Beautiful," and everyone would be invited to sing as the little pioneers, dressed as farmers and storekeepers and miners and such, marched around in a circle until the song ended, when they would line up along the back wall so they would be out of the way when it was somebody else's turn.

Wiley and me were on the verge of panic, worrying what we were going to have to do. Mr. Phillips hadn't told us yet, but he assured us that everyone would have a part—as if we were all worried we would miss out on our chance to embarrass ourselves in front of the whole town. I couldn't imagine what Jesse and Curt would have to do. But Mr. Phillips would come up with something.

23

When I got home that afternoon, I walked up the hill to Waters' cabin. I saw him out in the orchard, and I walked over to see what he was doing. He looked up when he heard me coming. "Hey, Justin," he said. "I was just fixing to gather some shoots for grafting next year. You wanna come along?"

"Sure," I said.

Waters led the way through the old orchard between the rows of trees. He stopped now and then to look at one tree or another. "These trees came back pretty good, didn't they? Got rid of the dead wood, thinned out all the extra branches and such, they made a pretty good showing. Be even better next year."

He had a little basket in his hand, and every so often he'd stop and cut three or four shoots off one of the trees. He bundled them together, tagged them with a metal tag he'd scratched the name of the tree on, and put them in the basket. When he had cut all he wanted, we walked back to the cabin. I sat on the porch steps while he carefully wrapped his cuttings in the moss he'd collected and placed them in his special spot under the porch.

When he asked me, "What you been up to?" I told him about going to see the mine with Wiley and about school. "Couldn't stay away, huh? I figured you'd get back there sometime. Didn't fall in the hole, I guess."

"I know you told me it was dangerous, but I wanted to show Wiley. It's about the most interesting thing around here."

"It's okay. You just puttin' your toe in to see how the water feel. But sometime the water be deep. Just remember — trouble never very far away."

I decided to change the subject and told him about Mr. Phillips and his pageant idea. I asked him if he would come see the pageant when the time came.

"Sound like somethin' to see, for sure. I'll have to think about that," he said. "I've never been to Glory, 'cept that night we came through on our way out to the ranch. I don't think Hal thought it would be a good idea. Maybe things be different now."

Since he had kinda brought it up, I told him about seeing the scar-faced man in town. Waters frowned. "That man gotta chip on his shoulder. I don't know what made him like that, but something turned him mean. People don't start out like that. Something bad happen to them, they just turn mean-mad, always lookin' for a fight.

"It don't work that way with everybody, though. Look at Hal. Came here, bought this place, was fixing it up for his Orla. Then she up and died. That kind of thing turn some people. It changed Hal all right. He kinda off people after that, easier for him to deal with horses and machinery instead of people. Left the ranch and went to work in the mill. Gave up on that dream he had. But he back here now. He gonna be all right."

We talked a little while longer till it started getting dark, and then I walked back down the hill to the house and washed up for dinner.

After dinner I tried to work the arithmetic problems Mr. Phillips had given us for homework. I wasn't very good with numbers, and it always took me a long time. He liked to give us at least twenty problems every night. It seemed to me that three or four problems would be enough to show him whether we knew how to do them, but he insisted that we needed to practice and gave us plenty of chances. He was probably right, but it just seemed like so many more chances to make even more mistakes. I spent so much time erasing the mistakes that all my pencils were worn down on the wrong end, and I usually had to copy the papers over before I turned them in because of the smears and tears.

I did as many of the problems as I could. I hoped Wiley had better luck with them than I had. Maybe he would help me finish them before we had to hand in our papers. I left spaces for the problems I hadn't done and tucked my paper inside the book so I wouldn't lose it. I listened to the radio until I fell asleep, wondering what Mr. Phillips had in mind for us tomorrow.

The next day I got to school a little early. We compared notes on the math problems, and Wiley showed me how to do some of the ones I gave up on. Some of the others were stumpers, though, and neither one of us had been able to do those. After we said the Pledge, Mr. Phillips said he had some more ideas for the pageant. Wiley and me looked at each other and groaned.

"After Tommy, Alice, and Aaron have finished their parade, then Wiley, you and Agnes will step onto the stage dressed as a pioneer husband and wife." Wiley looked at Agnes, then down at the floor. His face turned red. "Together you will turn to the audience and say a little poem I have prepared for the occasion. I have borrowed a little bit from Walt Whitman, one of America's great poets. I'm sure he won't mind." He smiled when he said that, looking up at us. Must have been something funny in there, but no one knew what it was. "Anyway," he said, "I will give each of you a copy so you can study it before the pageant.

"Then Bobby, Mary, David, Todd, Amos, and Anthony–you're their children."

Curt Spencer snickered from the back row. I looked over my shoulder and saw Jesse giving Curt the stinkeye. Mr. Phillips just ignored them. He was in full swing now.

"You will each come out on stage one at a time. You will each say who you are and then tell why you have come to Glory. You will be speaking for your families. You may decide what you want to say. Ask your parents if you need help. When all six of you are finished, Agnes and Wiley will take you, their 'children', and stand behind the little ones so everyone can still be seen on stage when the next ones come out."

Sooner or later, we would all have our turn in the barrel. Mr. Phillips was really warming to the idea of the pageant. Every time he talked about it, it seemed to get bigger and bigger. He was dead set on having his pageant, and we were going to be stuck with it, like it or not. I wondered what he had in mind for Annie and me, but I wasn't about to ask. I would find out soon enough. Whatever it was, I figured there was nothing to do but grin and bear it, but I was afraid there wouldn't be much to grin about.

The days were shorter now, and there was a chill in the air that hadn't been there a week or two before. The maples beside the school dropped orange and red leaves that swirled in the wind and piled up in the gutters along the streets and littered the school yard. The porch steps glittered with frost in the morning sun, and it was nearly dark when I got home from school.

By now Mr. Phillips had divided us into four groups. The littlest ones—Tommy Cochran, Alice Babcock, and Aaron Sykes—were about seven or eight years old. The middle group, the ten to twelve year-olds were Bobby Sadler, Annie's brother, Mary Garber, David Sykes, Todd Andrews, Amos Weatherby, and Tony Carvalho. My group was next and included Wiley, Agnes, Annie, and me. Because they were too old to fit in anywhere else, Jesse and Curt were by themselves in the last group. I had no idea what Mr. Phillips had planned for them. I figured just getting them to show up at the pageant would be an accomplishment.

Mr. Phillips started keeping each group in after school one at a time so they could practice their parts in the pageant. On days when our group practiced, Jesse had to stay after to look out after Agnes, and he was mad because that meant that he had to stay after two days and not just one like everybody else. Wiley and Agnes had a part together in the pageant, and Jesse didn't think much of that, either. Wiley was pretty embarrassed about the whole thing, but he was secretly pleased, too, since he really liked Agnes. I couldn't tell whether she had caught on yet or not. That girl didn't miss much. Maybe she was just waiting for Wiley to catch up.

On the practice days it really was dark when I got home. By the time I checked on the cows and made a trip from the woodshed to fill the box on the porch and split kindling for the kitchen stove, it was black dark, and the stars were out. I could do my chores by moonlight when the moon was full and the skies were clear, but most of the time I had to carry a hand lantern, and when it rained, I wore a slicker and rubber boots that sank into the mud as I slogged from one place to another. It was nice to come in from the cold and warm myself in front of the fireplace or sit on the hearth after dinner and work on my homework.

It was cold in my room at night now, even with flannel sheets on the bed and three or four blankets piled on top of me. When I went to bed, I got in, pulled the covers up to my nose, and put the radio headphones over my ears to listen to whatever program was on before I went to sleep.

25

Mr. Phillips had scheduled the pageant for Friday night, the week before Thanksgiving. There was no school on Thanksgiving and the day after, so he decided we would put on our show the week before. That way everyone could be with their families on the actual Thanksgiving holiday. We had each been sent home with a note inviting our families to attend the pageant. The little ones had their notes pinned on their shirts so they wouldn't lose them on the way home. We had made a big banner like the one that hung at the back of the stage to put up on the outside of the school, and Jesse and Curt had hung it from the bell tower. We had made posters to put in the windows of the stores on Main Street. Annie had been in charge of putting the posters in the store windows, starting with her father's grocery store.

Mrs. Travers had agreed to help with our costumes, and I got permission to stay over at Wiley's house the night before the pageant, so we would be ready when Friday night came. Uncle Hal had driven me to school and taken the car back to the ranch. That way, he and Waters could use it to come in on Friday for the pageant. I wasn't sure Waters would come, but I hoped he would. I admit I hadn't been too keen on the pageant at first, but we had worked on it for so long that Mr. Phillips finally had us hooked. I wanted everyone to come see it.

Before we went to sleep that night in Wiley's room, we went over his part in the pageant. Wiley had gotten his copy of Mr. Phillips' poem to study, and he recited it over and over, with me reading Agnes' part. It was pretty tough sledding for Wiley. I could see why Mr. Phillips had picked Agnes for the part, because she was such a good reader and all. I guess he thought Wiley's feelings for her would help him rise to the occasion.

Before school let out on Friday, Mr. Phillips told everyone to go home and have dinner early, get in their costumes, and be back at school by seven-thirty. The pageant was supposed to start at eight o'clock, but Mr. Phillips wasn't taking any chances.

Mrs. Travers was helping a lot of us with our costumes. Agnes and Jesse lived too far away to ride home and back on their horses, so they went to Wiley's house after school. Agnes wasn't sure whether her folks would come to the pageant, even though Mr. Travers had offered to pick them up in his Model T pickup. He said if they squeezed in tight they could all fit on the single seat, but Agnes wasn't sure they would come.

Mrs. Travers had made a big platter of sandwiches, and they were piled high on the kitchen table for everyone to eat so they wouldn't have to go hungry to the pageant. We were just sitting down to eat them at the picnic table out in the yard when Annie showed up at the door. Mr. Phillips was quite a matchmaker. He had paired Agnes with Wiley, who still blushed every time he looked at her, and then he had picked Annie to be my pioneer wife, which, though it made me a little nervous, didn't make me entirely unhappy. Jesse and Curt were there, too, but they mostly stood around looking bored, like they were too old for all this kid stuff. They were dressed nice, though, with clean white shirts and dark pants.

After we ate, Wiley's mother helped us get into our costumes. Most of the boys were pioneers, so they were getting by in their own overalls with plain work shirts underneath. Mrs. Travers drew moustaches and beards on them with a burnt cork to add some to the illusion. Wiley carried a double-bitted axe from the Travers' woodshed and sported a handlebar moustache, and I had Uncle Hal's bullwhip to carry and some daubed-on chin whiskers to add to my charm .

The girls wore calico dresses. Agnes had a pretty green one that looked nice with her red hair, and Annie wore a blue one. This was the first time I had ever seen Annie in a dress. Annie wore a blouse with a long skirt to school most days. She usually had a sweater, too, but sometimes she wore overalls, especially if the weather was wet. Annie always looked pretty to me no matter what she wore, but the dress added some color to her picture in my mind. Wiley's mother gathered the girls' hair and piled it onto their heads under white prairie bonnets that she had made for them. She tied the bonnets under their chins, and then she put a few extra freckles on Annie's face with an eyebrow pencil, but Agnes saved Mrs. Travers some time by wearing her own. Both of the girls wore flour sack aprons, which toned down the prettiness a bit. Agnes got a cast iron skillet to carry and Annie got a wooden pail to complete her outfit.

When it was time to leave, we all thanked Mrs. Travers and trooped out the front door, parading down the street to the school. We walked around to the back door, which led into the room used by the minister when he was in town. Another door led into the area behind the stage. Mr. Phillips had given us a tour earlier in the week, so we knew where to go and what to expect. Mrs. Potts would get the little ones settled behind the stage curtain and then hold them there while Jesse and Curt were out front showing people to their seats. Mr. Phillips had at last found something for them to do.

When everyone was seated, the boys would come back and watch the little ones, and Mrs. Potts would come out from behind the curtain and go down the steps to the floor and take her place at the piano. Jesse was supposed to keep the little ones quiet and in place until Mr. Phillips made his introduction to the audience. Mrs. Potts was going to play a little medley to give the audience a chance to settle down. When she finished, that was the signal for Curt to pull the curtain, and Mr. Phillips would come out to say a few words. We could hear all the people talking out front as the grownups filed in and took their seats on the folding chairs we had helped to set up earlier. It sounded like there were a lot of people out there, which made Wiley and me kinda nervous, though the little kids were prancing around and raring to go.

When the clock struck eight o'clock, Mrs. Potts hit the keys and started playing. When she was finished, the curtain parted a ways and Mr. Phillips stepped out onto the stage. He had dressed up for the occasion. He wore a gray suit with a striped tie, and when he raised his hands to get the audience's attention, you could see the red suspenders under his coat. Finally everyone noticed him, and the last of the conversations died away as they quieted down to listen to what he was going to say.

"Ladies and Gentlemen," he began, "Welcome to our Thanksgiving Pageant. I am Mr. Phillips, your children's teacher. As you know, these are hard times, and some of you might wonder what we have to be thankful for this year." After a pause, he said, "Well, I for one, am thankful to have this job." When he said this, a little wave of laughter rippled through the audience. "But when we reflect on our lives, I think we have many things to be thankful for. We can be thankful for the homes we live in, however modest. We can be thankful for the food we have to eat. But most of all, we can be thankful for each other, for our children, for the friends we see around us tonight.

"Some of you have lived here all your lives. Some, like me, are newcomers. There are many circumstances that have led us to be here tonight. There are many paths to Glory, and that is the name of our pageant tonight. I hope you will enjoy the show as your children trace their Paths to Glory!"

Curt pulled the curtain open all the way, and Mr. Phillips gestured for everyone to stand up as Mrs. Potts began to play "America, the Beautiful." Mr. Phillips started them singing, "Oh beautiful, for spacious skies," and pretty soon everybody got the idea and started to sing along. I'd never heard that many people singing all at once. It must be what it was like when the school turned into a church and folks sang hymns together.

The little ones, Tommy and Alice and Aaron, came out from behind the curtain and started marching around in a circle. Tommy wore overalls and had a red bandana tucked in his back pocket. He had on a brown cowboy hat and clomped around the stage in cowboy boots carrying a sign that said "farmer." Alice had on a gingham dress with a green apron over it and carried a sign that said "storekeeper." Aaron wore buckskin britches and had a canteen on a strap that hung from his shoulder. He wore a burnt cork moustache under a battered tan hat that seemed too big for his head. He carried a metal pan in one hand and a sign that said "miner" in the other. They kept marching until the folks singing got to "from sea to shining sea," and the music ended. Then they lined up along the back of the stage.

Wiley and Agnes came out then, holding hands. They looked out at the audience, and then Agnes said loud and clear, "Come, O Pioneers," and Wiley said, his voice quavering a bit, "Come, you western pilgrims." Then Agnes said, "Come from faraway lands," and Wiley said, "Walk or ride howe'er you can," and they both said, "Follow the path to Glory!"

There were two more parts, and they took turns speaking, saying the last line together. The two parts went like this:

> Come, O Pioneers,
> Bring your long rifles,
> Bring your sharp-edged axes,
> You will need them soon!
> Follow the path to Glory!
>
> Come, O Pioneers,
> Build your rustic cabins,
> Raise your families now,
> Build your noble dreams.
> Follow the path to Glory!

Agnes really belted it out for everyone to hear. All that leading of the Pledge of Allegiance must have helped her voice. Wiley was doing his best, but he couldn't hold a candle to Agnes for volume. He kept up with Agnes word for word, but I doubt if they could hear him in the back row. But he looked good up there with Agnes' hand in one of his and that double-bitted axe in the other.

When they had finished reciting, they stood apart from each other so their "children" could step out between them. The middle children came out then and stood in a line between Agnes and Wiley. Mary took a step forward and said, "I am Mary Garber. I have come to Glory to raise a family." Then she stepped back, and David stepped forward and said, "I am David Sykes, and I have come to Glory to build houses for the people to live in." After David came Bobby, who stepped forward and announced, "I am Bobby Sadler, and I have come to Glory to run a store to sell food to the people." Then Todd stepped out and said, "I am Todd Anderson, and I have come to Glory to raise cattle to sell to the store to feed the people." After Todd, Amos sort of shuffled forward, looked down at his feet, and said, "I am Amos Weatherby, and I have come to Glory to start a school to teach the children." Some of us snickered a little over that one, since Amos seemed to be the last person in the world who would want to become a teacher. I thought maybe he was teasing Mr. Phillips. Last came Tony, who stepped forward and said, "I am Tony Carvalho, and I have come to Glory to find happiness."

When they were finished, Wiley led Agnes and their "children" around the stage in a circle, ending up along the back wall, behind Tommy and Alice and Aaron. Then it was time for Annie and me to come out on stage.

We were holding hands just like Agnes and Wiley, but my hand was sweaty and kept slipping. Finally Annie took my arm, and we walked to the front of the stage and turned to face each other. Annie looked at me and said, "We have all come to Glory for different reasons, but we are all glad to be here. We have many things to be thankful for." Then she turned to face the audience, and I did the same.

"I am thankful for my mother and father, who take care of me," Annie said.

I looked out into the audience and saw Uncle Hal, sitting next to old man Weatherby. I looked around some more and finally saw Waters standing at the back of the room. "I am thankful for my Uncle Hal and my friend Waters, who take care of me," I said.

Then Annie said, "I am thankful for my teacher, who tries to help me learn. "

"I am thankful for my friend Wiley, who was kind to me when I first came to Glory."

"I am thankful for my little brother, who looks up to me, even if he is a pest sometimes."

"And I am thankful this is the last thing I have to say tonight," I said, and people laughed when I said that. Then Annie and I turned around and walked toward the rear of the stage. She went to the left and stood by Agnes, and I went to the right and stood next to Wiley.

Finally, Jesse and Curt came out dressed as themselves. They walked to the center of the stage, looking nervous and bored at the same time. Then they said together: "Many roads have led us here, and those same roads will one day take some of us to places far away. But wherever we go, we will always keep Glory in our hearts." Then Jesse and Curt stepped to each side, and all of us stepped forward so we were in a line at the front of the stage. Mrs. Potts played "America, the Beautiful" again, and everyone sang along. When we got to "and crown thy good with brotherhood, from sea to shining sea," we all joined hands and took a bow while the audience clapped and cheered.

When the clapping died down, Mr. Phillips stepped forward. He looked out over the audience the way he had looked at all of us that first day–like he was trying to remember all their faces. Finally, he said, "Thank you all for coming out tonight. I hope you understand why I am glad that I have followed my own path to Glory. I am proud of the children–your children."

After that Mr. Phillips dipped his head a little and swept his arm out to the side toward all of us on the stage. We all took another bow, and the folks clapped and cheered all over again.

After they had settled down, Mr. Phillips announced that there would be cider and donuts for everyone down at the Bon Ton.

Folks stood up to leave, and there was suddenly a lot of noise in the room, the sounds of greetings shouted across the room, of people talking, of chairs being folded and carried to their places. The little children ran out the back door, where their parents were waiting for them. Wiley's parents waited with the others and congratulated Agnes and Wiley and Annie and me as we followed the other children out into the night air.

26

After we had all had some time to pat ourselves on the back and listen to some of the parents tell us how proud they were of us, we all headed down toward the Bon Ton. Wiley's parents were ahead of us. Wiley and Agnes walked in front of Annie and me, holding hands. Annie took my arm and held it tight. She shivered a little and said how cold it was at night now.

We passed by the feed store and the gas station, both locked up for the night. Blinds had been pulled down in some of the shop windows. Most of the businesses in Glory closed around five in the afternoon, but there were lights in some of the windows upstairs. As we crossed the street, I noticed that there were more cars than usual parked along the street, their front ends nosed in to the curb. A lot of folks had come to see Mr. Phillips' pageant, and I figured he was crowing like Wiley's rooster behind those red suspenders.

Up ahead the Bon Ton was lit up like a house afire, and folks stood outside, waiting to get in. Down at the corner across the street, light spilled from the grimy windows of the Snug, and a bunch of tough customers stood outside, their hands stuffed in their pockets, slouching with their backs against the wall. Their breath escaped in ragged clouds as they talked. Some of them looked our way as we took our places in the line.

The Bon Ton had been changed around to make room for the pageant-goers. The tables with their black-and-white checkered tablecloths had been pushed against one wall, leaving more open space in the middle of the room. Orange and brown crepe paper streamers stretched from wall to wall above our heads. Paper cups and napkins were piled high on one table. Other tables held platters of donuts with all kinds of colorful decorations, homemade cookies, and small candy treats. At the end of the row, Annie's mother ladled out warm cider spiced with cinnamon into paper cups. The back door was open, and the other tables from the dining room had been set up outside. There were quite a few grownups out there, steam rising from the cups in their hands as they stood talking. Uncle Hal was out there with Sully and old Mr. Weatherby, who was leaning on his cane and smoking a pipe. Waters was out there with them too, standing quietly behind the others.

People were milling about in the middle of the room, talking with friends and neighbors, waiting for their turn at the refreshments. Tommy Cochran and Aaron Sykes, still wearing their moustaches, chased each other around the room, dodging people in the crowd. The grownups talked about the pageant and how nice it was of Mr. Phillips to bring everybody together like he had. Some of them said nice things to Annie and me as we waited for our turn at the refreshment tables. Other people talked about the weather or how cute the little ones looked marching around on stage. Most everyone seemed happy to be there, and it looked like Mr. Phillips had helped all of them find something to be thankful for.

After an hour or so, the crowd began to thin out as people began to take their leave and head for home. Annie and me had gone out back 'cause it was kinda hot inside, with all the people crowded together in the room. When she saw her parents getting ready to leave, saying good-bye to their friends, Annie gave me a quick hug and then kissed me on the lips, which took me by surprise. It was the first time I had been kissed by a girl other than Momma, and I didn't know what to do. She said, "Good-night, Justin," gave me the most beautiful smile I had ever seen, and then hurried to meet up with her parents. Before she walked out the door, she turned back, looked at me, and waved. I smiled and waved back. It was only later that I remembered how good she looked up close, even with her prairie bonnet, and how her breath smelled like cinnamon.

The parents tugged their children after them. Mr. Phillips stood at the door, thanking everyone for coming out, shaking hands with the parents as they filed out into the street. We left then, too, Uncle Hal and Waters and me and Mr. Weatherby, who had ridden into town with them to see the pageant. Some of the men were still out back, waiting as their wives helped put things to rights inside the Bon Ton.

Old Mr. Weatherby didn't move too fast as he leaned on his cane, so when we got to the street out front, most of the people had gone on ahead, and we were pretty much by ourselves as we headed back to the car. When they had arrived, Hal had parked the car near the school to make it easier on Mr. Weatherby, but now we had a ways to walk to get back to it.

There were still some men lurking outside the Snug, though some of them had changed places with the ones inside, and a few new faces had appeared. They all turned to look at us as we walked past on the other side of the street. One of them suddenly turned and went inside the bar. A few seconds later, the scar-faced man I had seen the other day stepped out, followed by two others. One of the others pointed at us, then said, "That's him, I told you I seen him before. That's Brennan–and he's still got that nigger with him!"

Black Hat and the others turned to face us. The slouchers pushed off the wall and stood with them as they marched into the street toward us. There were six of them altogether. They stopped about a dozen feet away from us. The man with the scar looked at us a long time before he spoke.

"So this is where you gone to, eh, Brennan? Took the money, took our jobs, and then run off with the woman and that nigger. Where you had 'em stashed all this time? It don't matter one bit. You're the one I'm after. Think you're some mighty hard-ass foreman, carrying that whip around, treatin' us like mules while you keep your hands clean."

Uncle Hal stepped forward, looking the man in the eye. "Listen here, Brady. I haven't done you any harm. You were drunk. You were about to do something stupid, and I stopped you. I didn't steal anything from you. The mill was going to close anyway. Times are tough all over. It was just a matter of time. If you'd thought about it, you'd know I'm right."

"Oh, I thought about it. Ain't been thinking about nothin' else since you run off. Ain't been thinking about nothin' else since we got canned and put out on the road. And now I'm finally gonna get a chance to do something about it."

Brady moved closer to Uncle Hal, and the other men circled around them. Waters made a move to stop them, but one of the men stepped out of the circle and pushed Waters in the chest with both hands, pushed him hard so that he staggered back, off balance.

"Stay out of this, nigger. We'll take care of you next."

Two of the men separated themselves from the crowd

and grabbed Waters, holding him back, watching as the men closed in on Uncle Hal. Brady took a swing at Hal, and he ducked under it, stepping back a little. He cocked his fists, and he and Brady circled each other for a bit. "What's the matter, Brennan? Not so tough anymore? Can't talk your way out of this, can you?" Hal turned away from a quick jab by Brady, then planted his feet, swung hard with his right fist, and caught Brady on the nose as he tried to turn away. Brady stepped back, surprised, but there was pure evil in his eyes now. I had never seen anything like it before, and it scared me so I felt rooted to the ground, afraid for Hal and Waters and me, afraid to jump in, but unable to run, either.

Brady faked with his left hand and swung hard with his right. I could tell Uncle Hal saw it coming, but he was too slow, and the punch struck him hard on the side of the head, and he went down. One of the other men kicked him in the ribs, knocking the breath out of him. Another stomped on his leg with his boot, and I heard something snap.

I ran toward the mob, shouting, "Leave him alone!"

Waters jerked loose from the men and grabbed me, pulling me back. "Stay out of this, Justin, they'll kill you." As he said this, the men holding him back earlier caught him again and dragged him back.

Another man pushed me hard in the chest, driving me backward. "Stay out of this, son. Brady don't care who's in his way when there's a score to settle."

Waters tried to get loose again, but the men holding him were too strong, and he couldn't break their grip. Brady straightened up, wiped his chin with the back of his hand, and came toward Waters. I heard him say, "Now it's your turn, boy," and then there was a big explosion behind the mob. Everything stopped as we all turned to look.

Sully was standing in the middle of the street opposite

the feed store. He was holding a shotgun in his arms. A line of men stood on either side of him, holding axe handles and pitchforks. "Stop right where you are!" He said.

The line of men moved forward as Sully advanced toward Brady and the others. He racked another shell into the chamber, the spent shell spinning out onto the street. Sully held the shotgun firmly between his hands as his men formed a circle around Brady and his thugs and held them in place with their makeshift weapons. Without looking away from the men, Sully said, "Justin, go get the sheriff."

I ran toward the sheriff's office, but I hadn't even reached the corner when the sheriff and another man came running toward me, almost knocking me down. Sully's shotgun blast had drawn them out before I could reach the office. When they reached the scene of the fight, the sheriff hollered, "What's goin' on, Sully?"

"Just helpin' you out a little, Max. This fellow here, this Brady, had some kind of beef with Hal Brennan. They had words. Hal tried to talk nice to him. Told him he didn't want no trouble, but Brady and the other men there attacked Hal, beat him pretty bad. We saw what was comin'. McManus over to the feed store let us in. We picked up a few things and then come out to stop it. I reckon you'll take it from here."

Brady stood there, red-faced, glowering at the sheriff and his deputy. A couple of Brady's gang tried to run, but Sully's men had them trapped.

"That's right, Sully. Jim, take a couple of these men with Sully and get them to help us walk these boys back to the office. Lock 'em up in the back. Thank you, Sully. We'll take care of it from here."

There was a lot of swearing, and one of Brady's toughs called Sully "a goddam nigger-lover," but the sheriff and his deputy and a few of the men with Sully got things under control and marched Brady and his cronies around the corner and out of sight. When I turned back, Waters was kneeling beside Uncle Hal. Mr. Weatherby stood next to him.

"How is he?" I asked.

"He busted up pretty bad," Waters said, "but I think he'll pull through. Look like the leg's broke, and his ribs are stove in. We need to get him some help."

The only doctor within miles was "Doc" Abernathy, the vet who mostly took care of the large animals–horses and cows and such. He occasionally treated cats and dogs, but they weren't his first choice. Someone went to fetch the "Doc," and he showed up in a short time. He put a splint on Uncle Hal's leg, and the men carefully loaded Hal into the back of the Doc's pickup truck and Waters sat with him, holding him up so he could breathe better. I remembered Waters holding Daddy in his arms on the log train when they brought Daddy down from the woods, and I was scared Uncle Hal was going to die, too. When they were ready, Doc drove them back to his office.

"Looks worse than it is," Doc said when we gathered around Hal at the Doc's place. "His bruises will heal. He's got a few cracked ribs, but nothing's punctured inside. It'll hurt to breathe for a while, but that will go away. The leg's the worst part. It's a clean break, but it's going to be a long time before he's back on his feet."

Doc gave Hal something for the pain while he set the bone and covered his leg with a plaster cast. He wrapped Hal's broken ribs with tape, and then he made him rest for a couple of hours. I walked back to get the car and drove it over to the Doc's office. We slept in the car for an hour or two before we drove Hal back to the ranch, dropping Mr. Weatherby off at his place.

The next day Waters and I were sitting in the kitchen, talking over what happened. Hal was still sleeping in his room.

"Do you know who those men were, the ones with Sully, I mean? I never saw a lot of them before."

"That's the funny part," Waters said. "They were all my customers, the ones on Sully's route that he delivered the applejack to, and some that heard about it from Sully and came out to the ranch to buy it directly from me. I call them the applejack gang.

"Sully invited them all to come to the pageant. And they actually came. Now, there's a man missed his true calling. Man's a natural born salesman. He could talk anybody into anything."

He looked me in the eye and smiled, "It just go to show you what good folks can do when they come together. Good folks can knock the horns off the devil—but sometimes they take a lickin' doin' it."

27

Our second Thanksgiving in Glory had passed without any notice at all. It was only six days after the fight, and Uncle Hal was still not doing much more than lying in bed and sleeping, especially when he had taken one of Doc Abernathy's pain pills. The Doc was used to knocking out horses, and I wondered sometimes what he had given Hal for his pain.

A couple weeks after the fight, Sheriff Max showed up at the house. I was stacking some wood on the porch when he drove up in his big black car with the white-painted doors. He stepped out and walked up to the steps. He had on his gabardine slacks and a dark leather jacket that didn't quite close over his stomach.

"Is Hal up to seeing a visitor?" He asked.

"Haven't had any but Doc Abernathy. Sully comes by with the mail, but Hal's still in bed most of the time."

"I think he might want to see me. Why don't you ask him?"

I let him in the front door and went in to tell Hal. He was awake, propped up with pillows, his broken leg stretched out straight. "Sheriff Max is here, says he wants to see you."

"Send him back here. I'm in no shape to meet him at the door. I want to hear what he has to say."

I brought the sheriff to Hal's room, pulled in a kitchen chair for him to use, and left the two of them together. I wanted to hear what he had to say, too, but I figured they didn't want me in the room with them while they were talking. But the door was open, and I stayed in the kitchen to listen.

"How you doin', Hal?"

"Doc Abernathy says I'm okay, but he's not the one with the busted leg. He says I'll be laid up for quite a spell. Justin is taking care of me all right, but I think the pain in my leg has made me a pain in the ass at the same time. I get pretty rough with him sometimes."

"He's a good boy, Hal. He's probably doing the best he can."

There was a pause, and then the sheriff said, "I came to tell you that you don't need to worry about Brady and his pals. I phoned the county, told them what those men did to you. We had plenty of witnesses who knew what those fellas intended on doin'. County sent a bus down, hauled them all away. They'll be wearin' stripes and gettin' their three squares in the pen for quite a while. You don't need to worry."

"I just wish I could have taught them a lesson myself. I guess I'm getting too old for all that."

"Men like that don't learn but one way. Bein' locked up for a while will give them plenty time to think."

Hal and the sheriff talked a while longer, but I left them to it and went back to stacking wood on the porch. I thought about what the sheriff had said. It had seemed to me that the pageant and the cider and doughnuts afterward at the Bon Ton were the only good things about Thanksgiving. We were all thankful that Brady and his men hadn't managed to kill anyone, but I felt a lot better knowing that they were locked up and wouldn't be coming back to Glory to bother any of us again.

Uncle Hal spent a long time on the mend. At first he just stayed in bed. His busted ribs made it hard for him to breathe, and his leg was hurting a lot. Doc Abernathy had set the bone, but it was still painful and wrapped in a plaster cast that didn't allow him to move around much. I made him meals, not very good ones I expect, but I could cook Cream of Wheat and scramble eggs. I could make sandwiches, and Uncle Hal ate a lot of sandwiches during the weeks that I played nurse and housekeeper. I didn't do as well with dinners, but we got by the best we could. Hal complained plenty, but not about my cooking.

Sully still came by once a week with the mail and Waters' newspaper, but he soon added groceries because I couldn't leave Hal by himself for long. Mr. Sadler boxed up enough food for us to get by for the week, and Sully dropped it off at the house on his regular day. He and Pearl had come up with the idea, and Mr. Sadler had gone along with it, saying Hal could settle up with him when he was on his feet again.

Since he couldn't get out of bed, Uncle Hal had to use a bedpan, which taught me a lot of things I didn't want to know, and that part wasn't much fun. He was always one to keep things to himself, but his present circumstances made that pretty much impossible. Hal was in pain and couldn't do for himself the way he always had, and it made him fretful and ill-tempered most of the time. We tried to get through it all without too much bickering, but we had our patience sorely tested at times.

Waters sometimes had to help me get Uncle Hal out of bed so I could change the sheets. He would pull him up and help him stand on one leg while I ripped off the old sheets and put the new ones on. I learned to make a bed pretty fast. I also learned to do the washing, which was a bit more fun than I thought it would be. Except for making the bed and such, I mostly got the outside chores. Uncle Hal liked to take care of his house, and he had always done the wash before.

But things had changed since he got hurt, and I was trying to keep both ends of the candle lit at the same time.

Electric power was making its way along the Glory Road. Waters had cut an article out of the newspaper entitled, "The Power and Glory," about when the electric streetlights went on in town, and most houses there had gotten electricity by now, but the outlying areas were still in the dark. According to the paper, big farmers in California formed what they called "co-operatives" to bring electric power to their farms, but the farms around here were small, and the farmers thought it would be too expensive. They weren't in any hurry to try newfangled things anyway. So we used our kerosene lamps and heated water in a copper wash boiler. But Hal had bought Orla a Maytag washer that more or less washed the clothes for her. You still had to put in the clothes and the water, but then you could kick the starter pedal, and the gasoline engine would make the clothes thrash around inside the big square tub. When it was finished, you had to run the clothes through the wringer on the side of the machine and hang them out to dry. That part wasn't so much fun, but I liked listening to the splashing water and the popping sound the little green motor made.

While Hal was mending, I stayed home from school to take care of him. It was kind of funny how I missed everyone in Glory. I missed the mornings on the road by myself. I missed Mr. Phillips and his spelling lists and the math problems that often stumped me. I missed the little kids that tormented each other, and I even sort of missed getting the stinkeye from Jesse and Curt. I missed Wiley and the Wednesday lunches at his house, too, but mostly I missed my time with Annie.

When she kissed me that night at the Bon Ton,

something had shifted in our connection to each other. At that moment she had told me how she felt without saying a word, and it was the best thing that ever happened to me. She had been my friend for a long time, but that kiss was a promise of sorts, and I wanted to see where it would lead.

It didn't look like I would be back in school until after Christmas, and I didn't know how I could wait that long to see her again. When I went to bed at night, I still said a prayer for Momma, but I often went to sleep thinking of Annie and that cinnamon kiss. Finally, I had an idea. I sat down one afternoon and wrote her a letter. I told her about the goings on at the ranch, about how I missed everybody at school. I told her how much I missed our time together, and asked her to say hello to everyone for me. It looked pretty dry on paper, but I hoped she would understand what I was trying to say. I wanted to write, "Love, Justin" at the bottom, but I couldn't bring myself to do it.

The next day, I waited till I saw Sully's truck come up the road. When he stopped to drop off the box of groceries, I went down the steps to meet him like I usually did. I asked him to wait a minute while I set the box on the porch. Then I walked back to the truck.

"Everything okay, Justin?" He asked.

"Yeah, everything's all right. I was just hoping you could do me a favor."

"Suppose I could–what'd you have in mind?"

"It's just, well, could you take this letter and deliver it for me? I don't have a stamp to put on it."

Sully looked at the letter, at the name on it, then looked up at me and smiled. "Looks like an important letter to me—I think the U.S. Mail can probably afford to help you out." He took the letter and put it in the leather bag on the seat beside him.

"Thanks a lot," I said.

"Not a problem, Justin. But you might want to lay in some stamps if you're gonna be writin' a lot of these." He drove off then, waving as he went around a bend in the road.

After a few weeks, Hal's ribs weren't quite so tender, and with a considerable amount of help, he could get out of bed and hobble around on crutches. He had an old robe that he put on and tied around his middle. Since he couldn't bend over to do it himself, I would get down on the floor and help him pull his slippers on so his feet wouldn't get cold. When he was all set, he would lever himself up, and then try to crutch-walk out to the kitchen, where he could sit and drink a cup of coffee that I had made for him.

He always complained about my coffee, said it was too weak.

"You got to take time to build a pot of coffee, Justin. You let the water run through the grounds, then you let it rest a bit. After a while, you run the coffee through the grounds again. Then you'll have a proper pot of coffee."

It was kind of like the way Waters got more alcohol in his applejack. I tried making coffee his way, and it came out strong all right. It was strong enough to peel paint and tasted about as good. It would practically take the enamel off your teeth. I couldn't figure out how he could drink that stuff, until one day when I watched him pour himself a cup. He only filled the cup a little over halfway, and then he filled the rest with milk. After that, he put in two teaspoons of sugar. Only by cutting it nearly in half with the milk could he drink it. And the sugar took the edge off the bitterness. When he tried that with regular coffee, it came out mostly milk and tasted too sweet. No wonder he thought my coffee was too weak. After that, I learned to pour my own coffee after it was first brewed, and then I brewed it a second time for him.

Sometimes he made it as far as the front room, where he could lower himself into his overstuffed chair and sit in front of the fireplace. He liked that better, but the heat from the fire made his leg itch, and he had a little wooden ruler that he would shove into the cast to try and scratch himself. After he had gotten better, and we were pretty sure he wasn't going to die or anything, it was kinda funny to watch the things he did to try to get by and make himself more comfortable.

When Hal first came home after getting hurt, I used to wake up in the middle of the night. I kept having dreams where I was running in the dark. Something was chasing after Momma and me. I couldn't see what it was, but I was really scared. I kept looking back to see what was after me, and a couple of times I tripped and fell. Every time I tripped, Momma got farther ahead of me until I was finally alone in the dark, and the dreaded thing was still coming after me. I usually woke up then, my head wet with sweat.

Sometimes I woke up because I had to go to the bathroom, or because I heard a noise and thought Uncle Hal was having some kind of problem. I'd get up, go to the bathroom if I had to, and then check on Hal before I went back to my own bed. The bedroom doors were both open to the hallway, and I could hear Uncle Hal snoring in his room. The snoring itself kind of bothered me, but at least when I heard it, I knew what he was doing, and I could relax. But sometimes he would be snoring away and all of a sudden the snoring would just stop, and there would be no sound at all coming from his room. I kept waiting for him to start again, saying "Breathe! Breathe!" in my head, and then just as I was about to throw back the covers and rush into his room, he'd snort and hack, and then the snoring would start all over again. After a few weeks of that, I figured he probably wasn't going to die, and I stopped worrying and started sleeping through the night.

Annie wrote back to me and kept me up on all the doings in town. Wiley and Agnes were apparently seeing more of each other. Annie said they usually sat together at lunch, though Annie often joined them. In the morning, Wiley waited for her where the horses were tied, and Annie sometimes saw them sitting on the porch steps before Agnes headed for home. Jesse tried to start a fuss when he caught them together there once, but Agnes put him in his place. I wished I'd been there when that happened. It would have been something to see. Agnes could hold her own, it seemed. Anyway, there wasn't any more trouble between them after that. Mr. Phillips had even made her his assistant, helping him with the younger ones.

Those letters made me feel good, but a little sad that I was missing out on everything. I really missed being at school. I missed Wiley and the others, and even with the letters, I missed Annie.

28

Christmas arrived only a little more than a month after Hal got hurt. No one was really interested in celebrating, but Waters came by with a tree he had cut, and we made popcorn and used a sewing needle and thread to make popcorn garlands that we hung around the tree. Waters came to the house on Christmas Eve, and we got Hal into his chair by the fire in the front room and made hot cider and played Christmas songs on the piano. I gave Waters a sign I had painted at school that said "Apple Cider Sold Here" and had a drawing that showed a red apple with a worm sticking its head out. Annie had helped me with the drawing, but I painted the rest myself. I gave Uncle Hal a cane that Sully had picked up for me at the Rexall in town. I carved his name on one side and put "Xmas 1937" beside it. Doc Abernathy had said he would need it to get around with when the cast came off.

Waters gave me a diary with my name engraved on the cover. He had ordered it from the catalogue with some of his apple money. He said I'd had some interesting experiences lately, and he thought I might want to write them down. Uncle Hal wasn't able to get around, so I didn't expect to get anything from him, but he had gotten Waters to order a fishing rod and reel from Montgomery Ward and keep it at his place until now. It looked to be a big improvement over the cane poles we'd been using, and I couldn't wait to try it out next spring.

The best gift of all arrived late Christmas morning when a car pulled up in front of the house. When I looked out the front window, I couldn't believe what I saw. Mr.

Sadler was getting out of the car, looking up at the house. The passenger door opened, and Mrs. Sadler got out, too. She reached behind the seat, and brought out a big wicker basket. What I noticed right away, though, was Annie looking at me from the back seat window with that wonderful smile on her face. She was wearing a close-fitting hat, and her dark hair peeped out and framed her face in a pretty way. When she opened the door and stepped out, I was dumbstruck. I had so much I wanted to say but I couldn't find the words.

"Well, don't just stand there," she said. "Help me with these things." She handed me a box tied up with string and grabbed a sack from the seat beside her. As we walked to the house, she looked up at me, smiling, and said softly, "I'm really happy to see you, too."

They had brought us a Christmas dinner with all the trimmings. Annie's folks had brought carrots and celery, ham and sweet potatoes, and Wiley's ma had made deviled eggs and sent along a loaf of fresh bread with apple jelly and a pumpkin pie.

"Where's your brother?" I asked.

"Bobby's visiting at the Weatherby's. Amos is at his grandpa's, and Bobby was invited over for the day. We'll pick him up on our way home."

When they had all trooped into the house, and the food was set down on the table, Mike Sadler looked around the room, then turned to Hal. "Where's Waters?" He asked.

"He was here earlier, but he's gone back up the hill to his cabin," Hal said.

"Well, let's get him down here to join the party!"

Hal looked at me and said, "Why don't you and Annie go see if he'll join us for dinner?

I couldn't wait to be alone with Annie. I grabbed my

jacket. Annie put her coat and hat back on and wrapped a scarf around her neck, and we headed out the front door. When we started up the road, Annie took my hand in hers, and we walked along, not saying anything at first. It was just being with her that I had missed so much. We passed the barn and started up the path to Waters' cabin. Annie stopped then and turned toward me. She put her arms around me, leaned in a little, and then kissed me.

"I've been wanting to do that since you got here," I said.

"Me, too… Let's go find Waters now."

Waters was sitting on the porch when we got to the cabin, reading the *Farm Journal*. He had a jacket on over his usual chambray shirt and dark pants. It was cool out, but he had found a sunny spot. Steam drifted up from his coffee mug on the porch railing. He looked up when he heard us coming.

"Hey, Justin. Merry Christmas! Who's that with you?"

"This is my friend Annie. Her father runs the grocery store in town. She and her folks brought us Christmas dinner. Everybody wants you to come down and join us at the house."

"I'm pleased to meet you, Annie. You a lot prettier than Wiley. Now I know why Justin like to stop by your daddy's store so often."

We talked for a bit, and then the three of us walked down the path to the road and up to the house. There was a wonderful smell in the air when we got inside. We hung up our coats and hats and walked into the kitchen. Uncle Hal had told Annie's mother where to find one of Orla's nice tablecloths, and she had spread it out over the old oilcloth we usually ate our meals on. They had also brought Orla's good dishes from the china cabinet. We had never used them before, and I was surprised to see them now.

I had looked at those dishes many times when I walked past the china cabinet. I liked the way they looked. The plates were kind of squared off on the corners. They were cream-colored with a black rim. On the left side there was a house with a red roof and some orange and black flowers in front and an orange sun at the top with a cloud and some birds flying past. The right side had a big tree that reached all the way to the top. There were orange leaves on the tree and more flowers at the bottom. The colors were more like fall than Christmas, but I knew how special they were to Hal.

"Orla called them her 'story plates,'" Hal told me once when I asked about them. "She said you could make up a whole story just by looking at them."

"'I like to think about who lives in the house and what they're doing. Is the sun setting or rising?' She'd say, and 'Where are those birds headed?' It seems silly now, but Orla liked those plates so much. I think of her every time I look at them." He took one of the plates out and handed it to me. "Turn it over."

The mark on the back said "Sylvania" at the top. Underneath was a sun face peeking up over the horizon. The sun had eyes with eyebrows and rays that fanned out above it. Below the sun it said, "J & G Meakin" and below that the word "England."

"Orla loved that sun peeking up like that. She said it made her smile every time she saw it."

If Hal let them use Orla's plates, I figured he must be feeling pretty fine. Annie's folks had been good to us. Everybody had. Daddy would have said we were "peeing high over the bush" today. It really was a special day.

The food had been laid out on the table. The celery and deviled eggs were alongside each other in a relish dish.

The ham and the bread had been sliced and laid out on platters, and the sweet potatoes and carrots were heaped in serving bowls. The pie rested on the drainboard by the sink, promising more goodness later.

Plates were passed, knives and forks clattered on china, and conversations sprang up as we dug in. It was a real Christmas dinner with friends and family–folks who had gathered together because they cared about each other. The only thing missing was Momma.

After dinner, Annie and I helped clear the table. Annie's mom set a pan of water on the stove to heat, and the men went into the parlor to sit and talk while their dinner settled.

"Why don't you two go outside and sit a spell while the water's getting hot? I don't mind. You've probably washed enough dishes by now, anyway. I'm happy to help. We'll cut that pie when you get back."

She didn't have to tell us twice. We put on our coats and went out back. It was a little cool after the heat of the kitchen, but the setting sun lit the clouds and turned them orange, and wisps of fog were hanging in the bare branches of the willows along the creek. It was a grand evening, and we sat outside the woodshed and watched the sun go down.

"I'm glad we came today," Annie said. "It's nice out here in the country. Seems like a good place to stay."

"It's okay, I guess. Most of the time it's all right—but it's only just me and Hal and Waters. We get along most of the time, but it's not like it used to be." And then I just couldn't help myself. I told her everything–about Daddy dying in the woods, about Waters and Momma and Flag and the men at the mill. I told her about coming to Glory, about how Hal took Momma away somewhere in case those men came after us and how he wouldn't tell me where she was. I told her how much I missed Momma and the old life we had.

"But if we hadn't come here, I'd never have met you. You're worth all the trouble we've been through." I couldn't help it, but my eyes were leaking a little, and I wiped my face with my sleeve. "It's getting cold out. My nose is running. We'd better go in."

Annie looked up at me and put her hand on my cheek. "Thanks for telling me all that. It'll be okay, you'll see. Daddy says 'hard times make us strong.' I think he's right about that. Let's go have some pie."

A couple of weeks after Christmas, Doc Abernathy took off the cast. Uncle Hal's leg had shriveled some, being in the cast so long, but Doc said that was what usually happened. Hal was supposed to take it easy at first and keep using the crutches a while longer. But when he could put some weight on it, he should work on walking a little at a time, using the cane. It would be a while, the Doc said, but he should eventually be almost as good as new, though he expected Uncle Hal would always have a limp.

I knew Hal was pretty tired of being housebound, and he was always fretting about his cows. I figured the barn would be his first destination when the weather improved and he was strong enough to make it clear to the barn on his own steam. I thought we would both be happy to see him out of the house again.

29

Spring started with a splash. For two solid weeks, it rained nearly every day. Some days it just poured, and the creek soon overflowed its banks, spilling onto the road in several places. I missed three days of school because the water was too deep to drive through. There was nothing to do but wait it out. Going outside meant slogging through the yard, which had turned to mush. My boots sank into the mud and made carrying firewood from the shed to the front porch a thankless task. The wheelbarrow sank so deep into the mud with the weight of the wood on it that I couldn't push it across the yard and had to make several trips, carrying the firewood in my arms instead. Uncle Hal fussed about the cows and made me put them in the barn during the worst of the storms.

We usually waited until the creek cleared to pump water, but when the water in the tank ran out, we had to pump from the creek, which meant that muddy water ran from the faucets in the house, the toilet looked like somebody had already used it, and taking a bath in a tub of brown water seemed just wrong somehow. The water was supposed to be dirty after you got out of the tub—not before.

I spent a lot of time listening to the radio, keeping up with the *Lone Ranger* and the *Green Hornet*. I even gave the soap operas a try, but the Barbours on *One Man's Family* didn't interest me much, and I didn't care whether "a girl from a little mining town in the West" found happiness with a rich Englishman on *Our Gal Sunday*, either. I even tried reading an old book that Sully brought me from Mr. Phillips. It was called *The Motor Boys over the Rockies* and was about three boys named Ned and Bob and Jerry. They were flying over the mountains in an airship called Comet, looking for Indian captives. I wasn't a very good reader, and it was pretty slow going. It wasn't going to rain long enough for me to finish that book, and I gave up after ninety-some pages. I gave it a good try, though. I didn't think Mr. Phillips would be too disappointed.

One morning the rain let up for a few hours, and I walked up the hill to Waters' cabin. Wood smoke rose from his chimney and flattened out on a little breeze blowing down from the north. He usually burned apple wood in his stove, and it had a distinct smell. He came out on the porch when I knocked on his door, and we visited for a while standing there.

There was a pretty good view of the valley from Waters' cabin. The bare trees stood stark against the sky, and you could see where the creek had flooded, spreading out over the flat land on either side. It was still out of its banks and would stay that way for a while before it would go down enough for me to drive to school. Waters put his boots on, and we took a walk down the road to see what damage the flooding had done.

The sky was gray, and the air was cold enough to make my ears burn, but it was good to be outside for a change. We walked along for a while, not saying much, just enjoying being outdoors, taking in the sights. Everything was different in the winter, especially when the creek was up. The trees along the creek, mostly willows and alder, had lost their leaves, and you could see across to the other side in places that were usually hidden from view in the summer. The valley seemed a lot bigger somehow.

Where the water had gone down a little, the land

was covered with silt, and green stubble stuck up here and there. Waters said those low spots would be good places for a garden, said Hal had suggested they might start a little truck garden along there in the spring.

"Hal saved enough money to get the ranch started again, but I think he runnin' a little short by now. The garden would bring in a little extra, give some more for ourselves, too."

I wasn't too keen on that idea, since I figured Uncle Hal wasn't going to be doing much on his bum leg, and I knew who was going to be tending the garden. But I understood what Waters meant. If Hal's savings were running out, we all had to pitch in and take up the slack. Maybe if he could find a tractor for me to drive, but I couldn't see myself out there with a hoe, pulling weeds in the hot sun.

We came to a spot where the river made a bend, and the road curved to follow it. It had flooded here, too, but the water had gone down some since then. A wire fence that ran along the road had trapped a lot of things behind it. Sticks and branches hung from the wire, and in one spot a dead deer was caught in the fence. It reminded me of the sad end Momma's Flag had come to.

Further along, we found an old redwood log that had floated up on the bank. The river had gone down and left the log beached at the edge of the field. Waters said we could come down in the summer and saw that log up, split it up into fence posts and firewood. That gave me an idea.

"Maybe we could talk Mr. Weatherby into borrowing his tractor for a while this summer. I don't think he does much farming anymore, but he's still got lots of equipment down at his place. I saw an old tractor in his barn, and there's a plow and discs and other stuff alongside the barn. I saw an old flatbed trailer down there, too. He did ask me about maybe cuttin' hay for him next season. Maybe we could work out a trade."

"Now you thinkin', Justin," Waters said. "We could make fence posts and firewood out of that log, maybe give Weatherby some of the firewood, trade him some labor at haying time for the use of his tractor. Hal's pretty good with mechanical stuff, could probably get that tractor up and running. Weatherby's turned out to be a pretty good friend to us. I bet we might work somethin' out."

"Wiley said he might give me some chicks when his hens started setting. It would be good to have some chickens of our own."

"Sure would. Get our own eggs and have us a chicken dinner sometime."

We talked a little more about our ideas as we walked back to the house. I said I would talk to Uncle Hal about it. The garden was his idea, and it would be good for him to have something more to think about besides his leg and those cows.

Waters spent most of his days during the rainy spell holed up in his cabin, worrying. He fretted about the apple trees, worried that if the rain kept up until the trees started to bloom, the rain would knock the blossoms off, and then the fruit wouldn't set. On the rainy days, Waters stayed in his cabin looking out the window at the rain coming down or reading the Stark Bros. catalog and old copies of the *Farm Journal*. I told him he could always read the walls again if he got bored, but he didn't think that was so funny. When I couldn't get across those deep-water patches on the road to go to school, it also meant that Sully couldn't get across them to bring Waters his newspaper, and he fretted over that until the creek finally went down enough so that Sully could get out with the mail. Waters was standing at the mailbox, waiting, when Sully finally made it through.

Even though it seemed like the rain would go on forever, Uncle Hal was in better spirits than Waters or me. One day he joked that he'd start building an ark any day now, if he could only figure out what a "cubit" was. I figured he was able to make jokes about it because he didn't have to go slogging through the rain up to his ankles in mud, but he was probably feeling better because he was healing now, and a little rain wasn't nearly as bad as what he'd been going through before.

Eventually, just like in Miss Garvey's bible story, God kept his promise, and a rainbow appeared. White clouds loomed on the horizon, and patches of blue replaced the gray skies that had hung over us in the past weeks. The end was in sight, and everybody's spirits lifted considerably. I discovered some new bone-jarring potholes on the road to Glory, but I soon learned to drive around them and got to school just fine. Uncle Hal was definitely feeling better, and Waters stopped fussing about his apples getting knocked off by the rain. Things were looking up.

When it had dried out a little around the ranch, Waters declared it was time to set out the new grafts on his All-American tree. While he cut the clefts into the ends of the branches, I held the basket with the grafts and handed him stuff when he needed it. He let me trim some of the cuttings to the right length after he showed me where to cut them, and then he reminded me how to shape the other end to fit the cleft. We wrapped the grafts and covered them with grafting wax to seal them when we were done. Waters put his arm around my shoulder, and we walked through the rest of the orchard, checking on the trees, looking to see how they were coming along, whether they had any pests, whether they were showing any signs of budding. Waters couldn't wait to be busy again.

30

It had been almost six months since that night outside the Bon Ton, and things had begun to return to normal. The hills had started to green up, the apple trees were budding out, and Uncle Hal was continuing to mend slowly. On warm afternoons, I walked out to the porch with him and saw that he got settled in the old rocker there. He liked to "warm his old bones" in the sun, he said. He didn't say much, as usual, but he wasn't complaining, either. He kept asking about his cows, and I kept trying to tell him they were all right. They were getting ready to calve in a month or so, and he was worried about them. The worrying probably kept him from thinking about himself so much. I figured the cows could probably get the job done without his help, but I understood how he didn't want to miss the big day. Doc Abernathy had assured him he would heal almost as good as new, but told him it would take a few weeks more.

One Sunday I took the Model A out of the barn and drove down to the house. I parked right in front where the path from the front porch steps led out to the road. Then I went inside. Uncle Hal was sitting beside the fireplace where it was warm. He had just finished eating the lunch I had made and brought out to him, and he was leaning back in the chair, looking like he was sleepy and about to take a nap.

"Come on outside, Uncle Hal," I said. "I've got an idea."

"What now, Justin? I was just about asleep. It's nice and warm right here."

"Just get your coat on and come with me. You'll like

this. You'll see."

He grumbled and complained a little, but I could see I'd finally gotten his attention. I got his hat and coat, helped him up, gave him his cane, and walked him out the door. When he saw the car parked in front, he said, "What's going on? What are you doing with the car?"

"Just wait," I said. "You'll like this. Come on."

He complained a little more, especially when I practically carried him down the steps. "Go a little slower, Justin. It ain't easy like you think. I'm movin' slower'n old man Weatherby these days. Where're you taking me anyways?"

"It's time you got out of the house for a little while. Besides, I know you want to look at those cows. You probably think I haven't done a good job taking care of them, so I thought we'd just drive down, and you could see for yourself"

When I finally got Hal folded into the car, I closed the door, and started the car. I turned around, and we headed down the road to the barn. It wasn't much of a drive, but Hal seemed to perk up as we got closer. He grabbed the dash rail with his right hand and pulled himself forward in the seat till his nose practically touched the windshield. I could tell he really wanted to see how his cows were doing.

When we got to the barn, I swung the car around so his side was facing the door to the barn where the cows went in. They were standing in the pasture outside the barn. When they saw me coming, they came over and stuck their heads over the fence, looking up at me expectantly. They were both heavy with the calves they were carrying and looked like they had swallowed a couple of saddlebags that were poking out from inside.

Uncle Hal threw open the car door and was trying to make his way out. I went over to help him before he fell and broke his other leg. With me holding one arm, he used his cane with the other and poked his way over to the fence. When he'd gotten settled and had a good grip on the top rail, I let go and went into the barn and filled the coffee can with oats and brought it out to where Hal and his cows were having a visit.

The cows came right over to me, of course, since I had been the one feeding and taking care of them for so long. I took out a big handful of oats and then gave the can to Uncle Hal. I held out my hand to the one cow, who started licking me with her raspy tongue. The other one saw the coffee can in Hal's hand and went for it like she'd found a new friend.

When the oats were gone, the cows stuck around a little longer hoping for more, and Hal scratched their ears, and looked in their big brown eyes, talking to them a little before they pulled away.

After a while, Uncle Hal patted my arm a little and said, "You done a good job, Justin. They look just fine," and he let go of the fence and started back to the car. It was about the nicest thing he had said to me lately.

When we got back in the car, we took a tour up and down the road. Hal hadn't been out in ages, and he looked out the windows like he was seeing everything for the first time. I knew he was enjoying the ride. I pulled over at the spot where Waters told me Hal and he had talked about putting in the garden. I told him about my idea to trade Mr. Weatherby for the use of his tractor.

"Good idea, Justin. I think maybe we could work something out."

I was a lot happier imagining myself sitting on a tractor seat instead of sweating over a long-handled hoe, and Waters had as much as said he would help with the haying. The hay would be cut long before his apples were ready anyway. Hal was warming to the notion of putting in a garden; I could tell by the gleam in his eye. I drove down the road a little further and showed him the log that had a promising future as fence posts and firewood, and then I turned the car around, and we headed back to the house.

The improvement in the weather brought other changes, too. Wiley and me still shared our table in Mr. Phillips' classroom, and his ma made us lunch on Wednesdays as usual. But Wiley and Agnes spent a lot of time with each other. Sometimes they sat with Annie and me at lunch, but when I got to school in the morning, Wiley was waiting at the fence for Agnes, not me. I sat on the steps, looking down the street, waiting for Annie. After school the four of us talked for a while before going our different ways. I often walked with Annie to the market, but her brother Bobby took the fun out of it, even when Annie told him to run ahead, so we could pretend we were walking by ourselves. Wiley waited while Agnes tucked her books into the saddlebag and waved as she rode off, watching until she was out of sight

Agnes and Wiley were off together a lot of the time when we weren't in school. His pa hadn't exactly followed through on his promise to teach Wiley to drive, but he had given him a horse for Christmas, a black mare that Wiley called Boots because of its white stockings. Agnes was teaching Wiley to ride. He said it wasn't quite as good as driving a car, but the company was a lot better. I slugged him in the arm for that, but I wasn't really mad. He and Agnes were happy together.

During the week I did my chores after school, but on Saturdays I usually got up early, straightened up my room, fed the cows, brought in the firewood, and took care of whatever Uncle Hal had asked me to do. After that, if nothing else came up I tried to find an excuse to drive into town.

Sometimes Uncle Hal sent me on an errand of one kind or another, usually to pick up something we needed at the feed store or Sadler's Market. Annie worked in the store with her father on Saturdays, but he would usually let her out for an hour or two if the store wasn't busy.

Most of the time we dropped in at the Bon Ton first. Annie and I both liked cherry Cokes, and we sat on stools at the counter while Billie made them for us. We tried to take turns paying for each other. Uncle Hal gave me a little money once in a while, and if he asked me to buy something in town, I usually got to keep the change. Annie's father paid her a little for working in the store, so she always had money when it was her turn, but it made me a little uncomfortable if I came up short.

A couple of times we went down the street to Wiley's house. But he and Agnes went riding on Saturdays, and they had already left by the time we got there. I figured Agnes got enough practice riding to school and back every day; she didn't need to ride on Saturdays, too.

But apparently Agnes was as good at teaching Wiley to ride as she was at helping Mr. Phillips with the little ones in the classroom. Now Wiley got up early on Saturdays when the weather was good, took care of his chores, and then saddled up Boots and rode out to Fowler's Rock on his own. His mom said it was okay as he long as he got back by dark.

A few times it was raining when I showed up on Saturday, and Annie and her mother invited me upstairs. Business was slower when the weather was bad, and Annie's father said he could handle things by himself. At first I thought they worried about Annie and me being alone upstairs together, but sometimes her mother would run downstairs to take care of something, and we were by ourselves for a while. After a few visits, Annie's mom seemed to relax a little, and

I felt more comfortable being there with Annie. They had a really nice apartment above the store, with a sitting room with windows that looked out on the street and a big kitchen with a round oak table and four chairs with cushions Annie's mom had made tied to the seats. We usually sat at the table and talked while we played cards or Chinese checkers. Her brother Bobby was kind of a pest, but Annie let him play with us for a little while, at least until he got bored or his mom saw how stinky he was being and sent him downstairs to "help Daddy."

Sometimes Annie or her mother would make a batch of cookies. Snickerdoodles were my favorites. I always volunteered to help. I liked to stir the stiff dough in the big green bowl they used. Annie mixed the sugar and cinnamon in a smaller bowl, and we would take turns scooping up the dough, rolling it into a ball and rolling the ball in the cinnamon and sugar. The smell of the cinnamon always reminded me of our first kiss at the Bon Ton. We had managed to get in a few more kisses since then, usually at the bottom of the stairs when Annie walked me down to the street as I was leaving.

Annie's momma always made me feel like she was glad to see me, and that meant something. She was Annie's momma, not mine, but I liked it when she was there. It was so different from being with Hal or Waters. She had a comforting way about her that made me feel like I used to when Momma was there to look after me. She and Annie's father had gone out of their way to help us after all the trouble, and I felt that kindness again when I was with them.

When summer came, Annie thought we could go out with Wiley and Agnes, maybe have a picnic or go swimming in the creek. When Annie talked about good things ahead of us, it made me feel like we weren't just passing the time together. It made me feel like she wanted to be with me. There wasn't much to do in Glory, but it was always nice being there with Annie.

One Saturday in the middle of April Uncle Hal sent me to pick up a sack of oats at the feed store. When I got back to the house, I saw him sitting in the porch rocker as I drove down to the barn to park the car. He often sat out there now when the weather was nice, but this time Waters was there with him, sort of sitting on the porch rail. I hardly ever saw them together, though I knew they talked from time to time—usually when I wasn't around. But they seemed to be having some serious kind of talk. Waters was leaning against the porch post with his arms folded across his chest, looking down at Hal in the chair. Neither of them even looked up as I drove past them.

I got the car parked and put the sack of oats in the steamer trunk. I was sliding the barn door shut when Waters walked past the barn and headed up the hill to his cabin. I raised my hand to wave, but he didn't look my way. I walked back to the house, wondering what I had missed.

That night, after dinner, Uncle Hal let me play the piano—actually asked me to play the piano. I took some of my favorite rolls from the music cabinet and played them through. I had worked up a sweat, and my legs were starting to cramp a little, and I had just about decided to quit. But when I started to put the piano rolls away, Uncle Hal asked me to play that *Rose of Tralee* that he liked so much. He hadn't asked for a long time, but I didn't think much about it. He had asked me to play it so many times before.

I put the roll on the piano, pulled the paper down, and hooked it on the bottom roller. I pumped the pedals up and down, and the notes started scrolling down. I played the whole song through and then, when it was over, I sat there for a while catching my breath. I looked over at Uncle Hal. His eyes were closed, and I thought he was asleep. I put the roll back in the cabinet and was about to leave the room. Just then, Uncle Hal opened his eyes.

"Sit down for a minute, would you Justin? I need to tell you something."

I sat back down on the piano bench, wondering what was up. Uncle Hal never just wanted to talk about anything.

"I need to tell you something," he said again. "It's not easy for me to talk to people. By now, I'm sure you've figured that out. But this is important." He paused for a bit. "You remember the night we left the mill and came out here to stay?"

I nodded. Of course I remembered that night. It was more than a year and half since then, but that night changed everything. How could I have forgotten it?

"That night—that night was terrible. I knew there was trouble brewing. After your daddy died, things kind of fell apart. Your momma was having a hard time. So were you. Waters was your daddy's friend, a good friend. He was trying to help you and your momma. He was having his own troubles, too. When your daddy was alive, everything was fine. He and your daddy stood back-to-back against the world, and they kept the world at bay. Nobody messed with them. Then your daddy died, and the world closed in on us.

"Your momma was alone, and Waters tried to help her, came to your place for dinner on Saturdays like always— trying to keep things the way they were before. I didn't like Waters at first, either, wouldn't have hired him if he wasn't with your daddy. I knew the other men wouldn't tolerate a Negro in the camp. They were a motley bunch, but I knew they didn't want him there. The first time they got liquored up there was bound to be trouble.

"By then I realized Waters was all right. I still didn't like him, but I knew he was good for you and your momma, was trying to look out for you in his own way. But then they killed Flag, your momma's pet. She loved that deer, and they took that away from her. I knew then that she was in danger, too. Other men didn't—couldn't understand how she and Waters talked in the cookhouse in the mornings. They saw him going up to your cabin on Saturday nights and drew their own conclusions about what was going on.

"So that one night, they caught him out and jumped him. Most likely they would have killed him if I hadn't stepped in to stop them. Hard treatment is the only thing people like that understand. It could easily have gone another way. I had never been more afraid in my life than when I was facing those men down. Only when we drove away from there could I relax.

"But I was still afraid for your mother. Some people at the mill knew I had this ranch. I was afraid they would come after us. I figured Waters and I could stand up to them if they came after us, although I may have been wrong about that. But I still worried about your mother. Killing Flag was a bad sign. So that night, after she put you into bed, I took her to another town far away, down past Glory—far away, where I hoped no one would find her. I never told anyone where she was. I didn't tell Waters, and I didn't tell you because I didn't want anyone to be able to force you to tell where she was if they came after her.

"Things settled down after we got here. Everything seemed to be fine. We'd all found something to do here. You were in school. Your momma was safe. But when those men came for us outside the Bon Ton that night, I thought I had been right after all to keep things to myself.

"I thought sure those men would kill me. Waters

stepped up, but it was too late. We were outnumbered. It would only have been a matter of time.

"Then Sully showed up with the applejack boys and saved us both. I didn't understand till then that we would be all right here. We had made a place for ourselves here. More than anything else, Waters had made a place for all of us. When those white folks stood up for Waters like that, I knew we would be okay."

"But what about Momma? Where is she?"

"She's all right, Justin. She's been safe all along. That's what Waters and I were talking about out there on the porch when you came back from town today. I never told Waters where she was before, and I was going to tell him today. But he already knew. He knew all along."

"But how could he know and not tell me? He never told me anything."

"Waters wanted to protect her, too. He knew how important it was to keep her safe. But he knew where she was just the same."

"How could he know?"

"You know how attached Waters is to his newspaper. Reads it front to back, cuts things out and pastes them on the wall?"

"So? What about it?"

"Think about it. Who brings Waters the newspaper?"

"Sully does. Why is that important?"

"Sully knows everything that happens up and down the Glory Road, all over the country. Waters asked him to look around, keep his eyes open. When Sully found out where your momma was, he talked to her, gave her a note from Waters. She's been sending him letters inside the newspapers ever since."

No wonder Waters loved that newspaper so much. It

all made sense to me finally. "What happens now?" I asked.

"Waters will write her, tell her it's all right to come back. Sully will deliver the letter. If everything goes right, Sully will bring her out the next time he comes."

So now I knew everything—at least I thought I did. At first it made me really mad. I understood that Hal knew where Momma was all along. He kept it to himself, thinking to save her from trouble. But Waters knew, too, and that cut a little deep. He hadn't told Hal, and I could understand that. But he hadn't told me, either. He had always treated me right: he gave me advice sometimes, but he let me make up my own mind about things. He made me feel like I wasn't just a kid. It was the only time he had ever let me down, and it hurt. I felt like somebody had socked me in the chest and I couldn't catch my breath.

I had a lot to think about when I went to bed after talking to Hal. I tried to sleep, but I had a hard time of it. I was surely at sixes and sevens over the news. When Uncle Hal started snoring in the other room, I finally got up, threw on my jacket, and went outside. It was a clear night with a full moon bright enough that I could see my shadow ahead of me on the road as I walked along. It felt like someone was walking with me.

I wandered down to the creek below the road. There was a place where the water made a bend around a big rock. I climbed up on the rock and sat, listening to the water rushing by and the sound of the crickets hard at work in the bushes along the creek. A mockingbird worked his way through his songbook, and once in a while a bullfrog let out its throaty rumble. It was peaceful and soothing somehow. I just sat there for a long time, sorting things over in my mind. After a while, I turned away from the creek and looked back at the ranch. I could see the light from Waters' cabin on the hill on one side and the glow from the lamp I'd left on in the house on the other. The barn was just a big shadow between the two. I thought about this place we had come to and how everything fit together. I looked at those two points of light and the darkness in between for a long time. The world was still turning beneath me, and I didn't know what to think.

After a time, I climbed up the bank to the road. I looked over my shoulder once and saw my shadow behind me. There had been so many secrets. Everybody had kept secrets. Hal had kept secrets. Waters had kept secrets. As it turned out, even Momma had kept secrets.

31

The next morning I got up and got dressed a little earlier than usual. I hadn't gotten a lot of sleep and figured I might as well get up and go feed the cows. I smelled coffee and looked into the kitchen. Hal was hunched over his coffee cup, looking half asleep, and didn't look up as I walked past and went out the back door.

It was still early, but the sun was up, and the grass sparkled with dew. The cows were waiting for me at the fence. I tossed them some hay and let them eat oats out of my hand. They looked at me with those liquid brown eyes and flicked their tails at some flies that had gotten up early, too. I thought I could learn something from the cows. They didn't ask for much and seemed pretty happy no matter what was going on around them. It could be raining or freezing cold, but they just stood there chewing things over. Sometimes, if the sun was a little too hot, they might look for a shady spot under a tree, but they always seemed happy where they were.

While I was studying the cows, I heard Waters playing his mouth harp. If the weather was good, he often sat out on his porch in the morning, usually warming his hands with a cup of coffee. Sometimes he'd set the cup on the porch rail if he was reading his paper, and once in a while he'd take that mouth harp from his pocket and play for a while. The sound always reminded me of when we were all together–Momma and Daddy and me–sitting outside the cabin on Saturday night, with Momma singing one of her songs and Waters playing along. Now it seemed so long ago and far away. I'd heard this song before. It was one I knew from the piano rolls

I had played for Uncle Hal. I recalled seeing the words as they scrolled down the page:

> Beautiful dreamer, wake unto me,
> Starlight and dewdrops are waiting for thee;
> Sounds of the rude world, heard in the day,
> Lull'd by the moonlight have all pass'd away!

If the moonlight could replace your troubles with starlight and dewdrops, the world would be a happy place for sure. I thought Miss Garvey would have liked that.

I walked up the hill to see Waters later that morning. He was putting the apple house in order, stacking up the empty boxes and lining up the crocks and barrels along the wall. When he saw me coming, he stood two of the boxes on end and sat down on one of them.

"Hey, Justin," he said. "Pull up a chair." I sat down on the other box and looked out over the valley below us. I couldn't bring myself to look at Waters right then.

"You look like you just found a hole in your best pair of shoes. Hal talk to you?"

"Yeah."

"Expect you got a few questions for me, then. Go ahead."

"Why didn't you tell me? If you knew where Momma was all along, why didn't you tell me?"

"I didn't always know. Hal wouldn't tell me where he took her, either. But I put Sully on her track, and he found her after a while. I been knowin' for a long time now, you right about that, and it grieved me not to tell you. At first I didn't tell you for the same reason Hal didn't tell me. It was safer for your momma if no one knew where she was.

"But after the letters started coming, I wanted to tell you everything. I was fit to bust with the news and couldn't talk about it with anyone 'cept Sully. I made him swear not to let on to nobody, and he kept his word. But your momma was the one kept me from telling you where she was. She wanted to protect you. She knew how worried you'd be, knew that if you found out where she was, you'd go looking to see her. Then the word might get out. I didn't say anything, even after the trouble in town. But after Hal's leg healed up and nothing more happened, I started working on him to tell you and let her come home."

I thought about it for a while, and it seemed like something Momma would do. I could see how she thought she might be protecting me, but I wasn't the same boy she'd left behind that night. A lot had happened since she'd gone away, and I could feel the changes in me. Waters had said my eyes were open wider now, and he was right about that.

"But where did she go? Where's she been all this time?"

"Your momma told me all about it in her letters. I know you remember Miss Garvey from the cookhouse. She your momma's friend, gave her that medal she wore sometimes. When those men come to warn Molly that trouble was brewin', Miss Garvey said there were rumors about the mill closing, and your momma asked what she'd do if it did close. She told her about the mission where she worked before, said she might go back there. And that's where Hal took her—the name and address of the mission on the back of the medal."

"Is she okay? She's been gone so long—long as Daddy has. Sometimes I felt like she was dead, too."

"She doin' just fine. Misses us all, especially you. But I been keepin' her caught up on the doin's since we got here. She know about you goin' to school, about the pageant and the trouble afterward. She know about Hal's cows and the applejack, too. Be happy to see us all again, get back to where she belong, she says."

Waters and I talked some more, and after a while I felt better. I still felt like I had been left out. Maybe Momma was right, and I was better off not knowing where she had been all that time. When I was little, she often told me, "Wait till you get a little older. You'll understand everything then." I guess she was right about that, but it wasn't as simple as she made it seem.

Things got more complicated when your eyes were open, and the road ahead was filled with surprises, like potholes that showed up after spring rain. It had been fun hunting for arrowheads and looking for fool's gold in the creek, but you couldn't do that forever.

32

April turned into May as we waited for Waters' letter to reach Momma and to hear back from her. It seemed like a long time, but school and chores gave me things to think about in the meanwhile. I told Annie the news as soon as I'd heard it. She threw her arms around me and hugged me tight. "I'm so glad for you. It's been such a long time. I know she's missed you, too."

I drove into town on Saturday and spent some time with Annie. We sat on the bench behind the store and talked for a while. I took her hand as we sat there and told her what was on my mind. "It's hard waiting. It makes me a little nervous, somehow. I've waited so long for her to come back. I kept thinking about how it would be, but things always seem to turn out different from what I expect."

"I know what you mean. That's happened to me lots of times. I think about how something will turn out, turn it over in my mind for a long time, think about all the possibilities, and then when it happens, it's never quite the way I imagined it would be. It's always different, somehow." She looked up at me then and smiled. "I remember how much I wanted to kiss you before that night at the Bon Ton. It seems silly now, but I'd been thinking about it for a long time, imagining what it would be like. I surprised myself when I actually kissed you."

"It was different than you imagined?"

She put her arms around me and looked into my eyes, smiling. "Yes, silly–it was better!"

Annie had pulled down the moon and put stardust in my eyes. No one had ever made me feel better. I just hoped she was right about seeing Momma again.

On the day Momma was supposed to come home, Waters and I walked through the orchard in the morning, just talking and looking 'round at the trees. They were in full bloom now, clusters of pink and white lining the bare branches. The All-American was in bloom, too.

Even the newest grafts were sprouting green leaves. One day Waters would have his coat of many colors that would be the envy of his neighbors.

Waters talked about planting more trees, new varieties that would bear more fruit and be there to carry on when the old ones finally gave out. I sat with him on the brow of the hill and looked out over the valley. The sun was out, the hills were covered in green, and new life was busting out all around us. This was a good place we had come to, willingly or not. Hal's dream had taken a wrong turn, but it had come out all right in the end.

Looking down the road, I saw a black speck moving this way. Then I heard the klaxon on Sully's Model T as it came into view. Waters and I got up then and hurried down the path to the road. As Sully came nearer, I saw there was someone beside him on the seat. It was a woman wearing a scarf tied over her dark hair. I hadn't seen her for nearly two years, but I knew it was Momma. She was holding something in her lap. When she got closer, I could see it was a baby, a toddler wrapped in a pink blanket. After he had pulled to a stop, Sully came around to help her down from the truck.

At first I didn't know what to make of it—Momma with a baby. Then it hit me like a slap in the face. I knew that Momma and Waters had kept the biggest secret of all. I wondered if Hal knew. Waters walked over to Sully and put out his hand. Sully took Waters' hand in his own, reached up with his other hand and touched him on the arm. They stood like that for a moment, and then Sully turned back to his truck. "See you again soon," he said. He fired up the old truck, turned it around, and headed back down the road, waving as he went.

I had waited so long to see Momma again, but I felt like I had been poleaxed like a steer at slaughter and just stood there taking it all in. I'd painted pictures in my mind of how it would be when Momma finally came back. I had missed her so much. I'd dreamed of running up to her, throwing my arms around her, and just melting into the comfort of her embrace, but this wasn't the picture I had painted in my dreams. I was dumbstruck and didn't know what to do.

Waters stepped forward then, Momma and he lost in each other's eyes. "Mr. Waters, meet your daughter. I call her Rebecca." I looked at Waters and saw a look in his eyes that I had never seen before, a soft look that came over him as he looked at the baby in her arms. Momma held the baby up, and Waters took her in his arms, held her gently with his strong brown hands, as if she might break.

"Come here to me, Justin. It's been a long time comin', this day. I've missed you so much." She put her arms around me then and held me tight. After a while she let me go, took my hands in hers and looked into my eyes. She took my arm and turned me toward the road.

"We need to talk," she said. We walked out to the road, looking out across the creek to the hills across the way.

"I'm so glad to see you, Justin. I've held you in my heart all the time since my goin' away. I hope you can forgive me for leavin' you, for keepin' everythin' secret. I was frightened. I made Waters promise not to tell, even though I knew how that would make you feel. I can see now, I needn't have worried about you."

We walked along the road, away from the house and the barn and Waters' cabin. I looked down at the road as we walked along, listening to her talk. "I know I left when you needed me most. You've grown up without me, and I'm sad for what we've missed out on together." She turned and looked at me then, reached up and pushed away some hair that had fallen over my eye. "You're not the boy I left behind that night, and I'm sad I won't see him again. You've grown since I left, I can see that. You're taller than me, now, and that's a surprise. But you've grown inside, too. I can tell by lookin' at you. You've got the look of your father in your eyes."

"Daddy was gone–and then you were gone, too. I didn't know where I was. I was just here with Uncle Hal and Waters. A lot of things happened that I wanted to tell you about, but I couldn't. After a while, it felt like you weren't ever coming back, just like Daddy."

"I'm sorry about that, Justin. I think I know how you feel. Your daddy was a good man. When he was gone, I was lost, too. There was a big hole in my heart. I had no idea how to go on. I wasn't much help to you in that time, though I knew you were hurtin'. I should have done more. I'm sorry.

"Waters was always there, always wantin' to be a comfort, but he was grievin' as much as you and me. After a time, he came to be more important to me than the loss I felt. We were good for each other. He will never take your daddy's place in my heart. Billy was my first love, taken away too soon, for sure. But Waters is a good man, too, and I know he's been good to you. He wrote about you in all his letters. He cares for you. Give us some time, Justin. We'll be a family again–you'll see."

"But what about the baby–Rebecca? She's gonna change everything."

"You're right, I'm sure. I know I could have left her at

the mission. Miss Garvey would have looked after her, found someone to take her in. But Waters wouldn't hear of it. A lot of our letters were about Rebecca and the trouble we had likely caused ourselves. But givin' her up to save ourselves is wrong. She is ours, and she belongs with us however it turns out. I hope you can understand."

It was a lot to take in all at once. I didn't know what to say. "What about Uncle Hal?"

"Hal won't be pleased, I know. But I think he might come around after a time. We're the only family he has, and family is important. I know he didn't like Waters at first, but he did the right thing in savin' him from those men at the mill, and I think he'll do the right thing again. He's a decent man. It will just take time. It's the rest of the world that will need pushin' back, I fear."

I remembered Wiley's surprise when he found out Waters was a Negro. But he had come around. So had Annie's family and Sully and his applejack gang. But I knew there were a lot more folks like Brady and his pals taking up space in the world, and I knew Momma was right about the rest of the world. I heard people talk even now, when they thought I wasn't listening. Somehow I knew that, for them, Momma had crossed a line by having Waters' baby, and there wasn't enough applejack in Glory to change their minds. We were headed for challenging times, I was certain of that. The toughest row to hoe wasn't going to be in Hal's garden.

When we got back, Waters was sitting with Rebecca on his lap. The wind was up, and apple blossoms drifted down from the orchard on the hill. Rebecca was giggling and reaching out, trying to catch them in her hands. A petal landed on Waters' cheek, and when she tried to get it, she grabbed his nose instead. Waters laughed at that and hugged her close, kissing the top of her head.

Momma sat on the grass, too, and patted the space between her and Waters. I sat between them and leaned against Waters' shoulder, putting my hand out to Rebecca. She clamped her pudgy little fingers around one of mine. She smiled with laughing brown eyes that reminded me of Flag.

Hal and Waters had known all along that this day would come. I'm sure their dreams had told a different story, too. But good things had come along with the bad and the unexpected. They were patient men who had found things to do in the meanwhile. Building a farm, starting a business, they had learned to look forward, to take a long view, believing good would come. I thought it must be easier to look back, to see where you've been, than to see where you're headed, but I had made some headway myself, I thought. I had made a new start on the Glory Road, too, without really knowing that I had done much at all. Mr. Phillips had the right idea. Everybody's life can be a path to glory. Sometimes there are potholes in the road and, as Waters once said, trouble was never very far away, but the folks you meet along the way make all the difference.

Momma was finally home. She and Waters had kept close with their letters while Momma was gone, but she hadn't told him about the baby until she was sure they would be all right together. He was happier about Momma and Rebecca than he ever seemed about his apples, so they would be all right, pushing back at the rest of the world. I hoped I could help with that. I had Momma back, and a baby sister, too. I had Uncle Hal and Waters and Wiley and Annie, too. I couldn't wait for Momma to meet Annie.

The Glory Road had led me to many a wonder. It had brought us all to each other and to a new home. I missed Daddy. But Hal and Waters were good men both, and I had taken much from each of them without even knowing. They taught me about things and people and the importance of patience. And Hal was right about Waters. More than anyone else, he had made a place for us here. He was quiet and kind and had taught me much about myself. Momma and he had grafted a new branch on the All-American, and I hoped the roots were strong enough to stand up to the storms ahead.

I had more to learn, some lessons harder than Mr. Phillips' arithmetic, for sure. But Annie's father said hard times make us strong, and I hoped he was right about that. I wanted to see the joy and keep the misery in the shadows. The road that brought us here stretched halfway 'round the world, and one day I would see where that part of it would lead me. But for now I was happy where I was. That was enough.

Acknowledgments

A number of folks have traveled with me along The Glory Road. I wish to thank them for their kindness and support. My thanks to Eileen Crowley, who bravely volunteered to read the first draft; to David Larison, the best brother an only child could wish for; to fellow writers, John Cox, Kitty Fassett, Davyd Morris, and William Weinreb, for their insights and helpful suggestions. And a special thank you to Tim Jollymore, my fellow writer and editor, without whose encouragement and critical guidance the story would not have made its way into the light.